HOLIDAYS SUCK!
PART 2

FANGSGIVING

ROBERT WINTER

BOOKS BY ROBERT WINTER

PRIDE AND JOY SERIES
September
Asylum

NIGHTS AT MATA HARI SERIES
Every Breath You Take
Lying Eyes

HOLIDAYS SUCK! TRILOGY
Part 1: Vampire Claus
Part 2: Fangsgiving
Part 3: coming soon!

WRITING AS M.J. EDWARDS
The Escort's Tale

DISCOVER MORE ABOUT THE AUTHOR ONLINE:
www.robertwinterauthor.com

HOLIDAYS SUCK!
PART 2

FANGSGIVING

BY ROBERT WINTER

To Les + Rich,

Love always wins!

Robert Winter

ROBERT RW WINTER

AN ORIGINAL PUBLICATION FROM
ROBERT WINTER BOOKS
WWW.ROBERTWINTERAUTHOR.COM

Fangsgiving
© 2022 Robert Winter

Cover Art
© 2022 Dar Albert

Series Logo
© 2022 Dar Albert

Author Photo
© Brad Fowler, Song of Myself Photography

Cover content is for illustrative purposes only and any person depicted on the cover is a model.

First Publication, December 2022
Print Edition

ISBN: 978-1-948883-12-2

ONE

Paul

PAUL SWUNG HIS heels as he perched on a mahogany table, eager for the moment his boyfriend opened the door to the crypt.

The steel slab mocked him with its bulk. So heavy that it would take at least ten humans to pull it open, it was further secured by the thick bar within that held it shut. The vampire who had originally built the home and crypt over one hundred years earlier had been pretty paranoid, Paul figured, to construct such a safe room for himself.

"C'mon," he muttered, glancing again at his wristwatch. The elegant hands of his Piaget indicated it was four twenty. Sundown was supposed to be at four twenty-seven that day; he'd checked. All summer, it had been torture waiting for Taviano, when the sun refused to set before eight-thirty at night. Then he'd lose their morning together because Taviano had to be back in his lair at the asscrack of dawn. Now, in November, after the clocks were reset, he could have so much more time with his Tall-Dark-and-Fanged man, with the nights growing still longer for a while. And Paul was greedy for every moment.

He pulled from his jeans pocket a mini candy bar left over from the Halloween party they'd hosted for the neighbors weeks ago. Biting into the slightly stale chocolatey goodness, he chewed thoughtfully. It rankled that, although they had been together for more than ten months, Taviano still would not permit Paul to sleep with him in the secured, windowless vault where he spent the day.

"But babe," Paul had tried, "your demon-thingy likes me even though it doesn't want to make me a vamp. It wouldn't eat me."

"We can't be sure of that," Taviano had answered in that low, sexy baritone, his Italian accent making Paul squirm. "We have been very lucky, yes. The demon that shares this body is aware of how important you are to me. Yet who knows what might happen while I sleep? I could crush you accidentally, or even bite you if my sleeping mind perceives you as a threat."

At the thought of being bitten, Paul shivered. Yet another thing Taviano had denied him so far. No matter how much he moaned and pleaded in moments of passion, Taviano wouldn't drink blood from him. It would be *super* hot, Paul was certain, to feel those needle-sharp fangs pierce his neck just as he was ready to come. Imagining the sensation, he had to shift as his cock stiffened in his tight jeans.

Well, he'd just keep at it until he wore Taviano down.

Watching a TikTok to pass the time while he waited, Paul snorted. A video of a little kid staring up at an aisle of Christmas items on a drugstore shelf, set to the song "We Need a Little Christmas", brought him an unexpected surge of melancholy. The idea of decorations going up a full week before Thanksgiving used to make him happy when he was younger. After the fiasco at his folks' house, though, the orgy of food and football on Turkey Day was a milestone he preferred to avoid.

Hard to believe sometimes that nearly three years had passed since his parents kicked him out of the house on Thanksgiving night. They hadn't even let him take a piece of pie, the bastards. No, just one little confession—*oh, I'm into dudes not chicks, can you pass the gravy?*—and Paul was suddenly homeless. The guy he thought was his boyfriend wouldn't let him move in to his dorm room, either, so Paul was also boyfriend-less.

Unable to deal with schoolwork on top of finding a job and a place to crash, he'd had to drop out of college. Three years on his own, with his grandmother and a few cousins the only family left to him, had shown Paul that Hell was being alone. He'd always stayed busy, of course, trying to keep a roof over his head, working with the LGBTQ+ teens at the homeless shelter, making what time he could to visit his nonna. But it wasn't until he'd found his vampire that he realized how hungry he was, for touch, for respect and affection. Taviano gave him so much of all that, unreservedly, and Paul was grateful for every moment.

He didn't really understand what Taviano got out of the deal, though. Paul was nothing special. Amusing plus good in the sack, maybe, but still an ordinary human with no special talent or smarts. He worried sometimes that Taviano would change his mind about staying in Boston, or his demon would grow tired of Paul.

Well, Nonna had always taught him to grab life by the balls, and so that's what he did. He grabbed on to every moment Taviano had for him by night. By day, he did his best to fulfill the vampire's trust in him. When Taviano had claimed the territory of Boston's North End and killed the vampire who previously ruled there, they'd acquired the decaying townhouse Paul immediately dubbed Castle Dracula. It turned out to be stuffed with cash and jewelry from decades of victims, none of it identifiable or returnable. And so together they'd come up with plans to put the treasure to good use, starting with the homeless shelter where Paul volunteered.

That reminded Paul, he was due to meet with lawyers about the foundation they were setting up. He made a mental note to get them to explain more about how the trust would work.

The steel door to the vault groaned just then, as the bar was raised and the massive thing was pushed open from inside. Paul's stomach tightened in excitement when Taviano stepped out from behind the steel door.

Immaculate as always, his dark eyes burned with intensity, and the scruff on his cheeks only highlighted his brooding good looks. He was about the same height as Paul, but his body was much more muscular. A black silk shirt stretched across his chest and over his cannonball shoulders. The black trousers he wore looked painted on, hugging his firm thighs and cupping his package just right. The gold crucifix Paul had bought for Taviano's one hundred ninety-sixth birthday dangled brightly at his neck.

"Bae!" Paul yelled, launching himself toward his lover. Taviano laughed as he caught Paul in midair and swung him around in a circle. When he stopped, his slid his hand up the back of Paul's head, combing through his hair as their lips met in a kiss. Paul tightened his arms around Taviano, knowing that no matter how hard he squeezed, his lover wouldn't mind. Taviano, on the other hand, had to be very careful not to crush Paul's ribs. It was one of the many things Paul loved about being with Taviano, that awareness of immense strength, kept under tight control to protect Paul from harm no matter how passionately they hugged or fucked.

"I probably reek," Paul said. "I biked over to the shelter and then rushed home when I realized how late it was. Should I go take a shower?"

Taviano growled sexily and pulled him close again. "I always love the way you smell. It doesn't matter if you're a little sweaty or fresh out of the bath."

"Sweet talker," Paul teased. "But you don't have to butter me up. You know I'm gonna put out."

"Is that right? You want to give yourself to me?" Taviano pulled their bodies tightly together. "Yes, I can feel that you do," he added, twitching his hips against Paul's erection. His own dick began to thicken, too, something Paul knew took a conscious act of will for the vampire.

He wriggled free of Taviano's arms and dropped to his knees, right there on the silk carpet that filled the hall in front of the crypt. He mouthed the growing bulge behind Taviano's pants. Eyes wide, he looked up at his lover as he unzipped Taviano's pants and fished out his thick, uncut cock.

"I'm already yours," Paul said, then took the head into his mouth.

Taviano gave a satisfying groan above him, and wove his fingers into Paul's hair. "Insatiable," he said softly in that deep voice of his that resonated in Paul's bones. The love in his voice was palpable. Paul couldn't believe this was his life—cared for by the most beautiful man he'd ever seen. He took more of Taviano into his mouth, bobbing his head and tugging on Taviano's balls as he sucked.

The essence of ichor stimulated his taste buds as Taviano responded to his oral skills. The substance that replaced all of Taviano's blood and other fluids tasted different every time. Tonight Paul got sea salt caramel on his tongue as precum. He moaned and stepped up his attack, wanting more of that delicious substance.

Taviano got the message and thrust gently, nudging the thick head of his cock toward the back of Paul's throat. Paul hummed his joy and pulled him closer with hands on Taviano's ass. He gagged slightly, backed off, then tried again. Taviano's head entered his throat, and he swallowed around it. Above, his vampire hissed with pleasure. Paul wouldn't release him, using his lips and tongue to bathe Taviano's cock with his love. It grew harder in his mouth and he pulled Taviano deep again, cutting off his own ability to breathe.

Taviano trembled, his hands tightened in Paul's hair, and he began to direct his bobbing. He fucked Paul's face, pulling back until just the head was on Paul's tongue before pushing back into his gullet. The speed built, Taviano issued a rare curse, and then the taste of caramel filled Paul's mouth. He swallowed Taviano's cum eagerly, drinking in the magic and the love that had transformed his life.

The ichor's effects began immediately. His head swam and the sounds of life swelled around him. With nearly a year's practice, he knew how to keep it from becoming overwhelming. Yet the flood of sensations thrilled him as much as the first time. He could feel every hair in Taviano's thatch, taste every slight vein and ridge of his dick, even smell the sheets that Taviano had slept the day in. Beyond their front door, the Boston evening thrummed with life and delightful chaos.

Paul released Taviano's cock and stood. He pressed their lips together and opened to invite in Taviano's tongue. They shared the essence of ichor, Paul's erection forgotten in the wonder of being with his vampire again.

He leaned away slightly, stared deeply into Taviano's eyes, and whispered, "Ti amo, angelo mio."

"Anch'io," Taviano responded, then said, "Mio tesoro. My treasure." He slid a hand down Paul's back, over his ass, then around to the erection straining his pants. "What would you like this evening?"

Paul shook his head. "Later. I want to let it build up. If you fuck me now, it's over too soon. I can't have unlimited orgasms like you."

Taviano chuckled. "Poor baby. We just have to make your two or three orgasms count then."

"You always do," Paul said, resting his head on Taviano's strong shoulder. "How did I get so lucky?"

"Good things come to good people," Taviano said. "You're the best mortal I've ever known."

"Yes, and you want me to stay mortal."

Taviano leaned back to look Paul in the eyes. "This again? You know my demon refuses to consider turning you."

"Is it your demon, though?" Paul asked. "I think you like the idea of me getting older than you. Soon I'll be your hot older boyfriend, then your daddy. At some point your granddaddy, if that's a thing. When you come to visit me in the nursing home, the other residents will say, 'Oh isn't it sweet his great-grandson still visits him'."

The words were teasing, but Taviano's eyebrows beetled together. "It's true that I would rather you never become like me. Your heart is full of light. But I would risk anything in the world to keep you safe, including this, if the choice were mine. It isn't, so instead I do everything an immortal vampire can to protect the fragile human who holds his heart."

"I know," Paul sighed, burrowing against Taviano's chest. "And I'll protect you with my life, however long that may turn out to be. Lucky everyone in my family lives a long time. Hell, Nonna is already eighty and going strong. Her mother was over a hundred."

"My love, what has brought this on tonight? Is there something else troubling you?"

After a pause, Paul said softly, "Thanksgiving is coming up this week."

"Ah." After a pause, Taviano asked, "Would you like to go

somewhere else for a few days? We could take a trip."

"There's too much happening with the shelter right now. But I was thinking it could be fun to ask Nonna and some of the cousins over for dinner the day after Thanksgiving. You know, a Friendsgiving?"

"I do not know what that is, but if it would make you happy, of course I want to do it."

Paul squeezed him tightly. "I'll talk to Nonna about it tomorrow. C'mon, let's watch a *Great British Baking Show* episode before you give me one of those orgasms you promised."

TWO

Paul

THE NEXT AFTERNOON, Paul emerged onto the city streets from the downtown offices of his lawyers. As he zipped up his puffed jacket against the autumn snap in the air, he couldn't hold back a slight groan. He was a bit dazed from all the information the lawyers had shared and the decisions they wanted him to make. More than that, he was downright uneasy.

He shivered involuntarily as a moment of cold dread pressed in on him.

Just the pressure from the lawyers, he figured. Glancing at his watch, he decided there was time to stop by his grandmother's before Taviano emerged from his crypt. A look around the streets showed that pre-rush hour traffic was already slowed to a crawl. Tempting though an available taxi looked, he'd grown up in Boston and was well aware it could take him forty minutes to go the two miles to Nonna's apartment by car.

Fortunately, a Bluebike rack less than a block away drew his attention. Paul swiped open the app on his phone to claim one of the shared bicycles, popped it from the rack, and peeled off in the direction of Boston's North End. Dodging selfish drivers and careless pedestrians, he maneuvered his way through the financial district. Distractions battled for his attention at every corner, but he fought them valiantly to keep his eyes and his focus on the insane traffic.

Even with trying to keep his mind on the road, Paul relaxed as he passed the corner of Hanover and Cross Streets. A pleasurable pulse, deep in his body, thrummed like a harp string as he entered the North End.

Taviano—or actually, the magical blood-drinking demon that shared his life—had placed an invisible tripwire around that small, densely populated pocket of land it claimed as its territory. The spell or curse or whatever was intended to warn any vampire that it had entered a claimed area, and to let Taviano know if said vampire failed to heed the warning. Apparently, it worked by resonating to the presence of ichor. It wasn't until he whizzed by the Eliot School, where Nonna had taught high school English and Literature until she retired, that he realized the sense of dread had gone just as he crossed the barrier. Between his Thanksgiving angst and decision-making, no wonder he'd been unnerved until he got close to home.

Sure, that's all it was, he thought as he parked at the Bluebike rack closest to his grandmother's apartment building. He blew on his hands, frozen from the ride, as he walked over to the entrance and pressed the button for Nonna's apartment. When she buzzed him in, he climbed the stairs to the third floor instead of pausing for the elevator.

Nonna waited for him at the open door, peering out into the hallway. Her cloud of white hair was carefully pulled back like it had been when she taught school. The thick blue housecoat she wore brought out her eyes, the same cornflower shade that people always said Paul inherited from her. At barely five-foot-two, she looked fragile and doll-like. If you didn't know her, you'd never think she was tough enough to survive teaching in the inner city for thirty years.

"Paulie!" Nonna exclaimed when she spotted him on the landing. "I didn't think I'd see you again so soon. You were just here Sunday."

He bent way down to kiss her cheek. "I had a little time before Taviano gets home so I figured I'd see whether you have any of those cannolis still."

She chuckled. "You're worse than a bloodhound. I put one aside the other night before you arrived and I've been saving it. I should have known you'd be back to claim it." She dragged him inside and kicked the door shut. "Go. Sit. I'll bring some tea and we can share it."

Paul ignored that, following her down the hall to the small kitchen. "Nonna, you didn't ask who it was when I buzzed downstairs. It could have been anybody."

She blew a raspberry at him. "I saw you coming up the street."

Paul looked at her warningly. "Did you really, or are you just saying that?"

She shrugged. "Okay, I'll be more careful. I've been in this neighborhood my entire life, though. I can't imagine anything happening here."

"And Taviano wonders why I'm so trusting. You're a bad influence."

"Nonsense. Who wants to spend their life afraid of saying hello to a stranger or opening a door? You never know who you're going to meet." She retrieved a white cardboard box from the fridge, then leveled a stare at Paul. "Besides, isn't that what happened with your young man originally? You brought him back to your apartment, a stranger. Now look at you. All but married and settled in that mansion. Would that have happened if I'd made you afraid of your own shadow? I don't think so."

Paul laughed as he lit the burner under her tea kettle. He'd told her a partial version of what happened that night, including how Taviano had rescued him from a mugging. He left out a few details, of course, like the fact that Taviano was a vampire, that he'd used his weird powers to break into the homeless shelter to deliver Paul's presents, that he'd battled a small horde of vampires after they tried to murder Paul, and defeated them to claim mastery of the North End. And he *definitely* couldn't tell her Taviano used to hang around with her own grandfather, Calogero, in the Old Country.

Yeah, there wasn't really a good way to bring any of that shit up.

"Okay, you're right. Except the married part. I told you, Taviano and I are just gonna live in sin."

"Che palle," she complained in the Italian she lapsed to when annoyed or excited. "What balls. I don't care that you're two men, you know that. And I love Taviano. He's so good for you, this past year. Such a difference in you, Paulie. Such growth."

She shook her head ruefully. "But I want to go to a real gay wedding. All your cousins get married out of St. Stephen's or St. Leonard's. The brides wear those damn white dresses like they haven't been screwing since they were teenagers. Enough already! I'm an old woman. I want to meet those boys from *Queer Eye*, or those gay florists that are always on the *Barefoot Contessa* show. How am I going to do that if you don't get hitched soon?"

Paul just shrugged awkwardly as he poured hot water into the pot. "Taviano's from a really conservative upbringing. I don't think he'd be comfortable with the idea of two men getting married."

"Then he's a stronzino. You tell that boy to get with the times or I will. I don't want him stringing you along, Paulie."

"Don't call him an asshole. He loves me and he's done a lot of stuff to make sure I'm taken care of."

"What, like money?"

"Nonna!" Paul protested. But then he relented. This was his grandmother; she might as well know. "Yes, like money. He put a lot of it in a bank account in my name. There's a couple of rental apartments, too."

"Oh." She processed that as she carried their tea and the single cannoli into her tiny living room. "Well, that makes me feel better." But she frowned as she cut the dessert into two pieces. "I never asked you before, Paulie. But you have to tell me. Is Taviano mixed up in a famiglia?"

"What, the mafia? No, that's crazy. I told you—Taviano inherited his money."

That was close enough to the truth, Paul figured. After all, Taviano acquired a large house and fortune when he killed the vampire who used to claim the North End as her territory. That was kind of an inheritance, right?

Nonna still looked skeptical, but she let it go. For the moment. Paul knew she'd circle back to the marriage thing eventually. To distract her, he barreled forward with the idea that had popped into his head when he was waiting for Taviano to emerge yesterday.

"So, I figure you've got plans for Thanksgiving already." Nonna looked uncomfortable, confirming that she was going somewhere that included her son and daughter-in-law, Paul's parents. As angry as she was about how they'd treated Paul, she couldn't bring herself to cut off her only son entirely. Paul got it. Anyway, he and Taviano had received invitations from some of his cousins for Thanksgiving dinner, so he didn't care that the one invitation he stupidly longed for never appeared.

He didn't.

"I wanna have you over the day after Thanksgiving. You and some of the cousins like Luca, and maybe Sofia if she and her husband aren't going away for the long weekend. Tony and Gretchen with their kids. We'll do a Friendsgiving." He poked her with his elbow. "Does that sound gay enough for you?"

Nonna chuckled. "It's a start. Of course, I'd love to come."

"Great! I need some of your recipes, though. I wanna make pasta fagioli, maybe a lasagna with turkey instead of ground beef."

She made a face. "That sounds terrible. The gravy will be too much. Better to do something like a turkey tetrazzini. Trust me."

They bandied about food ideas until Paul realized how much time had passed. He jumped up. "Oh shit. Sorry, Nonna. I just realized how late it is. Taviano will be back from, uh, work really soon. I like to be there when he gets home."

It had been the easiest story they could come up with, that Taviano worked all day in some kind of office. It was certainly easier than explaining that his lover slept in a dark lair all day, rose at sunset, guarded the North End all night, and returned to his crypt at dawn.

"Okay, okay, I'll email you some recipes," Nonna said, rising from her chair. "You hurry on home before it gets too late. Be careful, though. Did you hear about that boy they found in Fan Pier Park? Seemed like a wild animal tore out his throat. Terrible."

Paul drew up sharply. "When was this?"

"Mrs. Paolo told me about it when I saw her at the market today. I think they found him yesterday morning. Whatever did that could still be around. It's so strange, because everything has been so much safer lately. There was a story in the paper and everything, about the crime rate in the North End being at historic lows."

"I'll be careful," Paul said, unable to resist preening at the news Taviano's efforts had been noticed. Fan Pier Park was outside the North End, only just, but he wondered if Taviano knew about this killing. Assuming it was a vampire, that was pretty sloppy, to leave a body where it could be found. From what Taviano had told him, vampires were usually OCD about hiding the evidence of their kills.

He offered a silent prayer for the dead boy. Taviano had a strict moral code about his victims, refusing to drink from anyone who wasn't a confirmed bad guy. Other vampires, Paul understood, were far less discriminating.

Maybe it wasn't even a vampire. Were there werewolves around, too? Ghosts? He hadn't thought to ask Taviano before. Sometimes it still shocked him to realize that there really were creatures of the night, preying on mortals.

At other times, it shocked him how accepting he was of his vampire lover.

Whatevs. Taviano was an avenging angel, in Paul's eyes. He did what he could to keep the people of the North End safe from predators human and vampiric, and his heart was beautiful. Even with his magic, soul-roommate demon-thingy, Paul understood there was only so much one vampire could do. Still, he'd mention the boy in Fan Pier Park and see if Taviano wanted to look into the death.

On the street again, Paul debated whether to grab another Bluebike to get home. Taviano would be able to leave his vault soon, according to Paul's watch, but Castle Dracula was about twenty minutes away at a fast walk. The early evening had gotten darker much sooner than he figured. And Paul was greedy; he hated to miss a moment with Taviano. The bike would save him a few minutes so he hurried back over to the rack and fished out his phone.

That was when he heard the scream.

THREE

Paul

THE CRY SOUNDED high and frightened, and seemed to come from a girl. Paul whipped his head around, trying to figure out where she was. He probably wouldn't have been able to hear it except that all the ichor his body absorbed from Taviano supercharged his hearing, his eyesight, even his stamina.

"Please. Don't hurt me."

He tracked the sobbing voice to an alleyway about a block up. Paul heard a low laugh in response, and flashed to Nonna's story about the dead boy in Fan Pier Park. Surely it couldn't be a vampire here in the North End. Taviano would know if that was the case, wouldn't he? He'd be here already. The fact that he hadn't swooped in so far meant either the threat was human, or Taviano had not yet risen.

But if he wasn't up, no other vampire would be either. Right? *Right?*

The girl shrieked again, and Paul started running toward the alley. He darted in, wishing for some kind of weapon. He'd never had a reason to test what else ichor did to his body, besides sharpening his hearing and his eyesight. Oh, and healing him quickly like when he sliced open his finger cooking. Maybe he had some cool ninja powers now, like Taviano. Strength, or maybe speed. *Something.*

He skidded to a halt behind three men who had a young Latina girl backed up against a wall. One displayed a knife while his two buddies caged the girl in with their bodies. Goon One grabbed her black hair and hissed, "Nobody's comin', chica. Not that they'd help a spic like you anyway."

Goon Two chuckled darkly. "Should a' stayed out of here. Should a' stayed in your own country. Now that you're here, you're ours to play with."

"You racist shitheads," Paul yelled. "Leave her alone!" The trio of toughs turned to look at him, and he suddenly realized all of them were huge. He really should have picked up something to hit them with. "I already called the police," he lied, brandishing his phone.

Goon Two snarled, "Stay outta this."

"Walk away," the one with the knife added, gesturing dismissively with the blade in his hand.

Paul's stomach knotted. He'd been cut once with a knife; it had bled like a motherfucker. Ruined his favorite sweater. He balled his hands into fists and prayed that he had enough magic juice in him to heal a stab wound if this went as badly as he expected.

Adrenaline surged in his body and he roared. Maybe if he sounded like a crazy man, they'd run away. He charged forward, swinging wildly at Goon One who was closest.

A punch to his stomach knocked the wind out of him, and he doubled over. Goon One followed it up with an elbow to his back, which knocked him flat on the frigid concrete.

"C'mon, superpowers. Kick in anytime," he wheezed, trying to rise. Goon Two kicked him in the ribs, and he groaned. Their knife-wielding buddy laughed.

That made Paul furious. So he wasn't a trained fighter. He'd show them, just as soon as he figured out how to stand up. He grabbed Goon Two around the ankle and yanked him off balance. As the guy fell, his head hit the brick wall with a dull thud.

"Oh shit, boy. You're dead now," Goon One chortled. He pulled back his fist for a punch, and Paul knew it was going to hurt. He tried to move out of the way, but he was still winded and off-balance. The fist descended and caught him on the back of the head. Stars exploded.

He collapsed to the ground, ears ringing from the blow. Down on the filthy alley pavement, too aware of the stench of garbage and worse, he tried to sort through the sounds he suddenly heard. Something was whipping around the alley, the breeze of its lightning-fast movements stirring the trash and dried leaves that shared the ground with Paul. The girl gave a startled cry, there were muffled groans in deeper voices, and then a satisfying crunch that sounded like a bone breaking.

"Taviano," he sighed. It had to be. His lover had known he was in danger and come for him. He pushed himself up to his hands and knees and looked around for Taviano.

The tableau before him made no sense. The girl crouched with her arms covering her head, and what looked like blood spatters along her thick denim jacket. Goon One was stretched out flat and apparently unconscious, his leg twisted unnaturally. He was better off than Goon Two, whose arm lay several feet away from his convulsing body. The one with the knife lay on his back, hands dangling limply, head obscured by some shape crouching low over him. The sound that came to Paul's ear was unmistakable. The shape was drinking blood from the neck of the man on his back.

And it wasn't Taviano.

FOUR

Paul

"HOLY SHIT," PAUL cried out. "Who are you? You're gonna be in so much trouble."

The shape dropped the man and whirled to face Paul. Still in a crouch, fangs bared, blood running down its chin, it snarled.

Appearance meant nothing with vampires, but this one looked young. Male, black, and *very* young, to Paul's eyes. He was overweight, with a Harvard sweatshirt stretching across his stomach, worn jeans, and white sneakers, but Paul had felt him move like the Tasmanian devil in those old cartoons. A madness in its face made Paul shut up fast. The demon inside this vampire was in control, and that made it a threat to everyone around it. Maybe everyone on the street, too.

Paul got to his knees cautiously and extended both hands, palm up. "Hey," he said softly. "You really don't wanna hurt any more people. You're already in deep shit for coming to the North End in the first place. If you hurt the boss' boyfriend—that'd be me—you're gonna face the, uh, true death."

He hoped he had the jargon right. Taviano had explained a few things about vampire custom but Paul hadn't paid that much attention. He regretted it now as he fumbled for the words he could say to calm the demon before it decided eating Paul was a perfect way to challenge Taviano for the territory.

The vampire boy blinked several times, a red light in his eyes flickering and dying. His body quivered, but he didn't attack. Paul counted that as a win. The aches in his body from his beating had already begun to fade—*Thanks, magic cum*—but Paul didn't want to test how much damage it could cure.

The boy's now-human eyes widened in fear. "The North End? Is that where I am? Oh God." He looked around frantically. "I didn't know. I swear. A-and you know the Monster?"

Paul blinked. "The monster. What monster?"

"You said you're the boyfriend of the North End Monster."

"Now wait a minute." Paul was indignant. "Taviano's no monster. Don't you dare call him that." He stalked forward, righteous anger making him forget the danger.

The vampire boy's nostrils flared. "I can smell it on you. The vampire lord. The destroyer."

"Destroyer?" Paul had to laugh. "Taviano? Are we talking about the same vampire?"

The boy hesitated at Paul's reaction, then frowned. "I...I don't know. Are we?"

"Well, what does your destroyer vampire look like? Because mine is tall, Italian and *smoking* hot."

"I don't know what he looks like," the boy admitted. "I just know that the North End is owned by a vicious beast who kills his own kind indiscriminately on sight."

The urge to defend Taviano warred with Paul's curiosity. Curiosity won. "Wait, if you know about Taviano, why were you dumb enough to come into the North End? Didn't you feel the barrier when you crossed it? Even I feel it and I'm not a vamp."

"That tingling? Is that what that was?" The boy rose and began to back away, head pivoting left and right. "Is he coming for me now?"

Paul thought about that. "Maybe," he said. "I don't know if he's up yet." He smacked himself in the head. "Well, that was a stupid thing to confess."

Luckily, the boy didn't seem to pick up on the fact that Paul had just announced he was a free Happy Meal. "I have to get out then. Where...where do I go?" His eyes looked beseechingly at Paul, then flicked to the girl still crouching against the wall. Her face was pale; she had to be in shock.

"You don't know where to go to get out of the North End?" Paul asked, his fear completely dribbling away as he watched the vampire's grow. "You seem pretty new. Don't you have a, what do you call it, a sire?"

The boy shook his head. "No. The woman who changed me was killed the same night."

"When was this?"

"Three months ago."

"You've only been a vampire for three months?"

"I was coming home from school late one night and she grabbed me. Did this to me. Then another vampire came along and there was a fight. I watched him tear her apart and I ran as fast and as far as I could." His eyes widened and a red-tinged tear ran down his round cheek. "I don't know her name or why she did this to me, but I felt her die. It was terrible."

"So, you've just been trying to figure this shit out on your own?" Paul guessed. This kid was kind of like the residents of the shelter: homeless, confused and vulnerable.

Okay, he was also a deadly predator, but still.

Many questions burbled through Paul's busy mind, but the one that came out was, "How'd you learn about the North End Monster then?"

"I overheard two vampires talking about him. It seemed like they had just met and they were circling each other like tigers.

My passenger was all riled up. It seemed like there was something going on that I couldn't see, some kind of struggle with their minds. Then they kind of stood down. One asked about Boston's North End, and the second one said that the monster who claimed it is vicious and powerful."

Memories of watching Taviano kill two vampires on Christmas Eve popped into Paul's head. "Well, he can be, I suppose. But only if he has to be."

"Do you know how I can get away from him?" the boy pleaded. "I just—I don't want to die. Again."

"Well, shit," Paul sighed. He knew already he was going to let the kid go, but still he asked, "Why did you help me with those assholes?"

The boy looked at the bodies surrounding them and the terrified girl. "I heard her scream. I wanted to help her but then the thing that's in my body kind of took over. My passenger."

"Taviano calls it a demon. But hey, what's your name? I'm Paul."

"Malik."

"Look, Malik, I don't want anything to happen to you. But my bae isn't always in control either. He might kill you before I get a chance to put in a good word."

"I'll go," Malik said desperately. "Just tell me where is safe, Paul. Please."

Paul groaned. "You need someone to teach you the ropes or you're gonna get yourself killed. Maybe if I have a chance to talk to Taviano before he sees you, I can get him all calm and shit. Then he can tell you about being a vampire."

"Wo-would he do that? I have so many questions." Malik's voice was hopeful, desperate.

"Maybe he'll teach you. It's worth a shot." Paul frowned. "But where can we stash you until I talk to him?"

"I can do the hole thing. That seems to keep other vampires from noticing me."

"The whole thing?"

"Yeah. Where I make a hole in a rock or the earth to sleep in. Or to hide."

Paul blinked. "I don't know what that is. I mean, I've never seen Taviano do anything like that."

"Really?" Malik looked puzzled. "I just figured it out, my first night. Like this." He held a hand out over the filthy ground of the alley. His brow furrowed as he muttered, "Just a little bit so the passenger doesn't take over…"

As Paul watched, the ground stirred beneath Malik's out-stretched hand. He waggled his fingers and the earth began to ripple, then to boil. The pavement surged up and poured away like a fountain, taking dirt beneath it as well. In moments, a hole the size of a body appeared. Malik lowered his hand. "I get in, then pull the earth back over me. I figured it out the first night, when the vampire who killed my maker was after me. I just wanted to hide and the passenger somehow let me know about this. The other vampire didn't find me. So far no one else has either. Doesn't your, uh, Taviano do the same thing?"

Paul shook his head. "Nah. He's got these nifty tricks with the air, though. And he picked up some shit with fire last year too, but he doesn't do that so much."

Malik hung his head regretfully. "I have so much to learn."

A noise from the girl drew their attention. She had risen to her feet but her hands remained pressed to the brick wall behind her. She looked wide-eyed at the prone bodies of her attackers and then up at them. Her mouth opened as if to scream, but only a squeak came out.

"Hey, can you do the memory thing?" Paul asked desperately.

"What memory thing?"

"Oh man," Paul sighed and called up images of watching Taviano. "I think you look deep into someone's eyes, use a little bit of your magic and just *tell* them to forget, or whatever you want them to remember."

Malik looked nervous, but he approached the girl slowly, one hand outstretched toward her. "You're safe now," he said. Her eyes widened in panic and Paul couldn't blame her, with the carnage scattered at her feet. Although Malik's back was to him, when he spoke again, Paul heard the command creep into it.

"I want you to forget that you were attacked and what happened here."

The ichor in Paul shivered reflexively, and he knew Malik's demon was using its magic. He whispered, "Tell her something good to remember, so she doesn't get bad dreams about the attack."

Malik glanced back at him, then at the girl. "Okay. You were walking home, you went into a bookstore to read, and you lost track of time. The blood on your jacket, uh—" He sent a beseeching look at Paul.

"Someone tripped and fell. They were okay but skinned their palm and bled a bit. When you helped them up, it got on you."

"Yes. That," Malik said to the girl. "Remember that. Now you should get on home."

The girl blinked at him dazedly, her head bobbing as if she were about to fall asleep. Suddenly she pushed away from the wall and walked past them both, down the alley, and around the corner out of sight.

"Hey, that's really cool," Malik enthused.

"We need to do something about these guys, too," Paul said, looking around. Two were dead; the third was unconscious. "I shouldn't feel bad about these raging dumbfucks." Respect the dead and let God sort it out, Nonna had taught him. He sighed and reluctantly made the sign of the cross on himself. "What do you normally do with the people you kill?"

Malik shook his head. "I don't know what you mean. I sort of—go under when the passenger gets hungry. I can see what it does but I can't stop it. Afterward, I just get away as fast and as far as I can."

"Holy shit. Did you kill a boy in Fan Pier Park a few days ago and leave him?"

"I don't know. I—*it* did kill some guy in a park, but I don't know where I was. He was torturing this stray dog. It made me sick, to hear the way the poor thing whined and cried. I guess the passenger took over, and the next thing I knew the guy was dead. I used some of my blood on the dog and healed the things that monster did to it. Then I ran away."

"Ichor."

"What?"

"You said you used your blood. It's called ichor. At least that's what Taviano calls it."

"Okay. Ichor."

Paul glanced at his watch. "Oh fuck. Taviano will be up any minute. We've got to do something fast."

"Should I...?" Malik gestured at the hole he'd opened in the alley.

"Yeah, that's good. Make it big enough to put the two dead guys in it. It's kind of creepy that they'll just disappear that way, but I don't have a better idea. Wake the third one, heal him up, and do the memory thing on him. Look, I've really got to get home and distract Taviano. Can you take care of all that and then hide yourself? Meet me here tomorrow and I'll let you know if I've figured out a way for you and Taviano to meet without him ripping you apart." Malik blanched. "Sorry. That wasn't cool. I'm just really stressed about time."

"Go. I'll finish up here."

Paul turned to leave, then said, "Wait a minute. How is it you're out and about before the sun has fully set? Taviano says he can't tolerate even the tiniest bit of sunlight."

Malik looked at him uncertainly. "I coat my body with this tiny layer of silica. It's so fine you can't see it but it works to keep the sun from touching my skin. Figured that one out all on my own."

"Good job. Okay, tomorrow. Same time. And probably best if you don't eat anyone else until we talk again."

"I'll try to keep the passenger in control. Since it fed some tonight, it should be okay." Malik began to expand his hole in the earth.

Confident that the boy's vampiric strength would be enough to deal with the corpses, Paul turned to hurry home. Two steps, and he staggered. The feeling of dread in his blood surged, slamming into him with a vengeance. Gasping, he finally realized it wasn't nerves but the ichor in his body, silently screaming a warning.

Paul looked around wildly, unable to tell which way to run, suddenly certain he had to get out of there and that it was too late. He had time to yell to Malik, "Tell Taviano!"

Then something landed with a thump in the alley behind him. Huge, strong hands grasped his shoulders before leaping into the gloom, bearing Paul away.

FIVE

Taviano

TAVIANO SWUNG OPEN the door to his lair, then paused, surprised and a little disappointed. Paul wasn't standing there. Almost every day for the past ten months, his mortal lover awaited him with a leap into his arms and a kiss. Sometimes a warm towel, or a cup of tea, would be waiting as well. Paul throwing himself at Taviano, confident his lover would catch him, was Taviano's favorite moment of the day.

He scanned the townhouse with all his senses. Maybe Paul was on his way down to the basement where the crypt was located? No off-key singing or scuff of feet in sneakers reached his ears, though. He could smell apples from a bowl Paul had placed in the entryway, chocolate from Paul's stash of Halloween leftovers, and the musky body wash Paul used when he showered. But the house felt eerily quiet.

Taviano's demon radiated a slight unease.

Could Paul be mad at him? Just yesterday, he'd again brought up the idea of being turned into a vampire. Then, after the lovely sex before Taviano went out to patrol the streets, they'd had that small but recurring argument. Paul wanted to sleep with Taviano in his lair. Just as he had since December, Taviano refused to permit it.

In the early years, when he'd been forced to travel with his maker Bronislav, occasionally he'd wake to find a dead human there, his throat ripped open or crushed in Taviano's grip. That wasn't a risk Taviano was willing to take, even for his fearless and stubborn Paul. Taviano loved him, more deeply than he had thought was possible between two men. It was something Taviano had never even dreamed of in more than one hundred seventy years of his vampire life. Paul had gifted him with his companionship. His joy in life. His generous love. He'd even given Taviano back the ability to attend Mass, once he'd proved that Taviano wouldn't burst into flames if he entered a church.

And with all those gifts, he'd given Taviano a purpose, too: Hunting the streets of the North End, protecting the innocent where he could, and feeding on those who would do evil. When he got home, there was Paul, waiting.

The mortal sins kept adding up, of course. Taviano's Catholic upbringing and his training to be a priest left him unable to ignore the continuing damage to his soul. With each attack, he knew he did wrong. Even his time with Paul was selfish in so many ways. Paul was pure of heart, and Taviano worried every day that he risked putting out that light. Add vanity to his list of sins, then, because he couldn't resist telling Paul about his escapades, just to see the happiness in his face.

"My own superhero," Paul said more than once.

Taviano had considered many times seeking the confessional, or at least asking for counsel from the parish priest at the nearby Catholic church. He frequented it when a Mass was held during his nighttime existence. Now that the days were short again, it was much easier to go to an evening or pre-dawn service. Attending church did much to ease his troubles. Sometimes Paul came with him, but his lover hadn't been raised with the kind of devotion Taviano felt.

If he did try to talk to a priest, though, what would he say? *Bless me, Father, for I have sinned. I truck with a demon, and I love a man. I have taken innumerable lives. What act of contrition may I perform to save my soul?*

Ridiculous. Taviano sighed. The burden was his to bear. If his demon was correct and they were truly immortal, then perhaps his day of judgment would never come anyway.

But immortality held its own punishment, didn't it? His sweet, naïve lover had such romantic notions of Taviano's existence. The idea of sentencing Paul to his endless nights horrified Taviano, even as he dreamed about what it could be like, to spend years, decades, centuries and even millennia together. Yes, as Paul had said last night, unless he were turned, he would grow old and eventually die, leaving Taviano alone while Paul ascended to Heaven. Taviano wouldn't even have the fantasy of one day meeting Paul again after his death, because he was surely doomed to Hell.

Fortunately for his guilt, he could truthfully answer that his demon was unwilling to make Paul a vampire. It was odd, though. Whenever Taviano tried to engage his demon on the subject, the refusal was swift, definitive and, sometimes, just a bit afraid. No matter how much he tried to probe, however, his demon gave him no explanation.

Nor did the demon give him a reason now for its unease. Unease that built into fear and then burst into panic as Taviano felt the presence of two vampires in his territory.

Eyes closed, he let his senses flow out, searching for the intruders. There! One was standing still, the other was moving toward it, very fast. He turned, rotating to face the vampires' direction, and then nearly shouted in horror. Paul—*oh Dio! No!*—was also there, right next to the stationary vampire and in the path of the second one.

Panic became fury as Taviano tore up the stairs and out of the townhouse, running through the gloom-darkened streets of Boston so fast he might have been flying. All his senses were focused on the intruders. The moving one raced toward Paul at a speed that rivaled Taviano's. With a growing sense of doom, he could hear Paul's heartbeat, a sound he would know anywhere. Paul was calm, for some reason, even though he was right there with the first vampire.

The second was closing in. It would reach Paul before he did.

Taviano ran faster, his demon roaring soundlessly in his head. The unknown, racing vampire was nearly upon Paul. He heard his lover yell, "Tell Taviano!" and felt the intruder change course, carrying Paul away with him, his heartbeat ratcheted up in fear now.

Taviano matched the new course to run after them. Was the fiend trying to get out of his territory with Paul? As fast as the vampire was, Taviano was getting closer. He was narrowing the distance. He realized then that the vampire was heading toward the Charles River. Surely he could catch them at the water's edge. Demon-speed propelled him forward. He was three blocks behind. Two. And then—

The other vampire disappeared from his senses, along with Paul.

Taviano stopped running abruptly, straining to hear, to *feel*. He had never encountered anything like that disappearance before. It was as if the vampire had stepped into a soundproofed room and slammed the door shut. Taviano couldn't sense it anywhere. Nor could he hear Paul's heartbeat any longer.

"Paul," he whispered into the night, praying his lover could somehow hear him. "I'll find you. Don't worry, my love. I'm going to get you back!"

The only clue he could think to follow was the vampire Paul

had been with before he was grabbed up. He ran back to the original location he'd sensed, an alleyway it seemed. He froze.

Three men lay on the ground, one alive, two dead. There was blood on the brick wall and on the ground, but it didn't smell like Paul's blood. A large hole in the concrete looked as if it had been scooped out by a giant hand.

He stood rigidly, calling on his raging demon's magic. For once they were united in their focus. Paul. Nothing mattered but Paul.

With the power rising up in his heart and spreading to his arms, his fingertips, his eyes and ears, Taviano could feel the vibrations of the ward he'd placed around the North End. Two breaks had left their trace, one small and somehow tentative, the other recent and purposeful. His demon pulsed its certainty to Taviano: The larger, more malevolent presence was gone from the territory, but the second one...

Still present, somehow.

Quivering with his need to do something to find Paul, Taviano nonetheless willed the demon and his tense body into stillness. With a solemnity he would have found as a seminarian before entering church for Mass, Taviano let the streets of Boston speak to him.

The bodies on the ground. A severed arm, flung away.

The echo of Paul's smell, already beginning to fade in the night air.

Another presence, weak but supernatural. A presence that left dust motes drifting around the mysterious hole in the alley. And more dust motes that drifted... Yes!

He shot out a hand into loose earth near the back of the alley, grasped a body in a shirt, and hauled it from beneath the ground where it had tried to hide.

"What happened here?" he bellowed into the terrified face of a vampire child.

"Don't k-kill me, please," the child begged. "You're Taviano, right? Paul said t-to tell you, to tell you—"

"To tell me what?" Taviano roared. "What did you do to Paul?"

Surprisingly, a sense of calm washed through his tense body, causing his fingers to loosen their grip on the boy.

His demon. Forcing him to stand down and, what was more bizarre, not chafing at the presence of another vampire.

All right. Fine. For the moment, he would comply. But if this vampire had hurt Paul...

Taviano set the terrified boy on his feet, made sure he was steady, and stepped back, hands spread in what he hoped was a gesture of peace.

Jaw clenched, he made himself speak in a softer voice. "Please, if you know anything that will help me find Paul, tell me."

The boy—well, Taviano now realized he was probably about eighteen or nineteen—still looked sick with fear. "I-I didn't mean to intrude in your territory, Sir. Uh, your lordship? Sire?"

"I'm Taviano."

"Right, um. I'm Malik."

"Malik. Fine. Why are you here, and what happened...?" He gestured expansively at the small massacre that surrounded them.

The boy looked guiltily around at the severed arm, the dead bodies, the unconscious man whose heart still beat. Taviano would have to deal with that soon, but he didn't trust himself to let out even the smallest bit of his demon's magic.

"Okay, so, uh...I heard a woman scream and I thought I could help, see?" Malik swallowed hard as he visibly steeled himself to answer Taviano's questions. "But when I got here these guys were whaling on, um, Paul." Taviano growled, and Malik took a step back.

"Go on."

"My passenger, oh wait, Paul said you said it's a demon? *It* took over and started, uh, stopping them. The bad guys." Malik's voice grew steadier and faster as apparently he decided Taviano wasn't about to drain him dry. "Then Paul shouted we were in the North End, and I knew about you, the North End Monster, see? And Paul said maybe you'd teach me about being a vampire so I was hiding the bodies and Paul said he had to get home to you and then"—Malik's voice slowed and dropped to a whisper—"*he* came."

"He?"

"The scariest vampire I've ever seen. My passen—uh, demon started screaming at me to run, and I think Paul felt it too because he was looking around all wild-like. Then this huge guy just dropped out of the sky, glared at me, grabbed Paul and took off. Paul yelled to tell you, and that was it. They were gone. I knew you'd come here so I hid but you found me."

Frustration welled in Taviano as he parsed through Malik's fear-soaked rambling. Of course Paul had tried to fight three mortal muggers. Stubborn, careless of his own safety—Taviano groaned in frustration. He prayed to the God he was sure rejected him that Paul was all right.

"Tell me what the vampire looked like," he ordered.

"Uh, white dude, huge. Maybe six-five? Six-six. Brown hair, kinda bushy. And the wildest mustache and beard I ever saw. Like, maybe what they call muttonchops? But sticking way out. Odd pants, kind of blousy and tucked into boots. His belt had these studs on them."

"Eyes?" Taviano asked, but he already knew.

"Black and burning. It was like, I could see flames there somehow."

"Bronislav."

"God bless you."

Taviano frowned at Malik. "That wasn't a sneeze. I think the vampire that took Paul is Bronislav. My maker."

"Whoa. But like, why take Paul? Why not just kill him right here? It's not like I could have stopped—"

Malik choked off at the snarl Taviano heard himself make.

"I don't know why he took Paul, but he will regret it. Back up. Tell me everything that happened before I arrived."

SIX

Taviano

MALIK'S STORY WAS distressingly short, and left Taviano with no idea how to proceed. After more than a century, why had Bronislav tracked him down now?

They had been in some town in Sweden with a small military garrison when Taviano could finally stand it no longer. It was deep in January, the ground and buildings covered in snow and ice when they arrived. Bronislav had a particular hatred of Swedish soldiers, and he'd dragged Taviano to the barracks building. The beast inside Bronislav seemed to revel in the vampire's barbarity, while the one inside Taviano kept warning him *not yet not yet not yet*.

The sentry outside had his throat crushed before he could cry a warning. Those sleeping inside had no clue that death lurked at their door. Bronislav had forced Taviano into the barracks with him. The barrier magic that would have safeguarded a home against vampirekind was absent in a space like the dormitory that no one could truly claim as their own.

"Stand there at the door if you are too cowardly to let your beast run free," Bronislav said contemptuously. "Let no one escape. If a cry goes up, be assured my beast and I will feast on this entire town."

Taviano had nodded, resigned. He had seen this violence play out many times over the years since Bronislav found him and turned him into a vampire. The carnage Bronislav wrought sickened him, and he was exhausted from fighting back the urges of the beast inside him to join in. Taviano had to drink blood to live, but he'd discovered he didn't have to kill. Yet death seemed to be what Bronislav's demon—and Taviano's—craved.

Four heartbeats inside the barracks led Bronislav to his prey. He could have taken them in their sleep, mercifully, but that wasn't what he enjoyed.

"Wake up, wake up, little soldiers," he cackled in Russian, rampaging through the small building to drag the four stunned men into the central room. One pushed himself to his feet, taking up a fighting stance. Bronislav darted in and the man screamed as his arm broke. Another scrambled toward a rack of weapons until Bronislav knocked him down and snatched up a sword. He rammed it through the soldier's hand, pinning him to the ground like a butterfly. The third opened his mouth to call for help but Bronislav slashed at his throat with sharp fingernails so the soldier fell to the ground instead, gurgling horribly as he clutched the remains of his vocal cords with a bloody hand.

The fourth ran straight for the door. Perhaps in his terror he didn't see the second vampire, but he ran right into Taviano's arms. Taviano held him against his body, feeling the warmth of the man. He could hear the blood surging in the soldier's body, driven by a heart pounding with fear. His demon stretched luxuriously in his head, preparing to savor the kill.

"Let go," Bronislav called, lifting his red, dripping fangs from the neck of the soldier who had tried to fight him. He threw the body across the room so it knocked over a table. A lamp left burning fell to the ground and its oil spread as it ignited. "This is what we are. What we do." He pulled the sword from the hand of the soldier he'd pinned, and studied the blade where it dripped rubies of blood.

The rising fire seemed to kindle something in Taviano. The scent of death in the air, the violent disregard of precious lives, the quivering terror of the man in his arms—he could bear no more.

"Go," Taviano said, pushing the soldier he held through the door.

"So it's come at last," Bronislav chuckled darkly. "My blood-beast warned me you were growing more rebellious."

He threw the sword in his hand with dazzling speed, straight at Taviano's heart. Without consciously deciding to move, Taviano dodged the blade and heard a *thunk* where it sank into the wooden jamb.

Bronislav fell into a crouch, ready to grapple. "I warned you that if you let the alarm go out, I would slaughter the whole town. Remember when I kill them all that it is your fault for disobeying me."

"They are innocent," Taviano cried out in anguish. "None of them have harmed you or given you cause for this evil."

Bronislav laughed. "The uniforms change, but these are the same soldiers I fought in the name of the Tsar Piotr. The borders change, but men do not. I have seen children burned, women raped, old men disemboweled for sport by this kind. What I do to them isn't evil but justice."

"Lie to yourself as much as you want," Taviano retorted, "but these soldiers are generations removed from your war. They are children of God and the violence you do to them is the work of the Devil."

The flames from the broken lamp had begun to spread along the barracks wall. Outside, shouts had gone up and he could sense people massing. Bronislav would tear through the defenseless townspeople like a scythe if he allowed it.

Demon, he thought at his bloodbeast. *Aid me now. Help me right the atrocities I have been party to for fifty years.* He received no answer, nor did he expect one, but neither did he feel resistance.

Even now, Bronislav didn't think him capable of fighting back. Surprise was his only weapon. He leapt over his maker's head, landed like a cat and lashed out with a foot that caught Bronislav in the back of his thigh. A bone broke and Bronislav cursed in Russian.

The leg would heal in moments but Taviano used the distraction to snatch a piece of burning wood and hurl it at Bronislav. The flames caught his clothes and ignited.

Rage distorted Bronislav's face as he whirled to face Taviano, heedless of the fire surrounding him. Instead of consuming the vampire, the blaze fanned out on either side of him, forming fiery shapes that looked like hands. They darted toward Taviano.

From somewhere deep in his damned heart, he called forth a tremendous gust of wind. With a roar, the gale met the flames and extinguished them, then tossed Bronislav against the opposite wall.

Momentarily stunned, the vampire fell to his knees and shook his head. Taviano found he had grasped the sword lodged in the door jamb. He pulled it free and whirled, slicing across Bronislav's face. Blood-infused ichor poured down from his slashed brow and cheek.

Bronislav put up a hand in a claw, beginning to draw more of the fire to him, but Taviano got to him first. He slashed and stabbed, leaping back from a fist or kick, then descending again and again.

The beast inside him exulted at the violence. It wanted to kill, to drain, to consume the very demon that resided in Bronislav's body. It pushed Taviano to move faster, now swiping at Broni-

slav's eye, now kicking his knee so it snapped. In moments, his
sire lay at his feet, ichor draining from a hundred cuts, bones
jutting hideously through burned clothes.

The walls were sheets of dancing fire now, the soldiers Bronislav hadn't had time to kill had rushed out, and the town square
was filling with men armed with swords and pikes.

Taviano's chest heaved as he stood over Bronislav's broken
form. He could leave his maker now, but the vampire would no
doubt heal and take revenge on this town. He could kill Bronislav
as his bloodbeast demanded, but the idea repulsed him.

Snatching the defeated vampire by the neck, he stretched out
a hand toward the wall farthest from the growing crowd and let
his demon *push*. Wind roared through the room, pulling the
flames behind it until it hit the weakened wall and broke through.

Taviano sped forward, Bronislav in hand, and headed for the
nearby forest. He dodged trees as he ran and ran, until finally,
miles from the town, he found himself at the edge of a frozen
lake. He ran out onto the ice and stopped at the center. With his
fist, he smashed down, splintering ice several inches thick, until
he had a hole big enough. And then he threw Bronislav's body
into the water.

"Your fate is in God's hands now," he whispered, and said a
prayer for the dead and wounded soldiers they'd left behind.
Then he ran on, knowing only that if Bronislav survived, Taviano
needed to be as far away as possible. He'd gotten lucky with the
element of surprise, but he couldn't count on that again.

SEVEN

Taviano

TAVIANO'S HEAD SWAM with memories as he stood helplessly in the alley. Was Bronislav in Boston to seek revenge? And why now?

He drew his attention inward, trying to commune with his bloodbeast. Its anxiety seemed…off. It wasn't afraid of Bronislav, that much was clear. At the mere thought of a fight, Taviano could feel it preen. The other demon essences it had absorbed, at Christmas and once later when a vampire tried to challenge Taviano for the territory, had increased its power immeasurably.

But would Bronislav know how strong Taviano and his bloodbeast had become? Perhaps he thought taking Paul would weaken Taviano, or force him into a trap.

That would work, of course. Taviano would do anything to keep Paul safe, even sacrifice his immortal life, if that was what it took.

His demon rebelled at the idea of giving in to another blood-beast, yet underneath that, Taviano could sense they were coming into agreement on one thing: Paul must be saved, at any cost.

"Um, Mr. Taviano, sir?" Malik's tentative query brought Taviano back to the horrors of the alley. "That guy is starting to wake up, I think. Wh-what should I do with him?"

True enough, the man who still lived was emitting low groans. Impatiently, Taviano gestured at the dead.

"Finish disposing of these. I'll deal with the last one. And please, just call me Taviano." He was on the man in a blink, hauling him to his feet. The man's eyes fluttered open, terror growing as he raked his gaze over Taviano's face.

"I don't know what you thought to accomplish here," Taviano growled, "But it's over. Forever." Tendrils of power crept into his voice as he eased just a bit of his rein on the demon. "Women terrify you. They are powerful, dangerous, to be obeyed without question. Never again will you be able to think of one sexually. They are so far above you that you can only hope to be noticed." He shook the terrified man. "Go and find the women in your life. Confess the wrongs you have done, in thought and deed. Abase yourself and beg for forgiveness. No, not even that. For the chance to *seek* forgiveness."

He pushed the man away disgustedly, and watched him stumble, then regain his feet. "One last thing," he said viciously. "You will remember what happened here tonight, but you will never be able to reveal it in word or deed. Yet you will know that I am here, and that I can find you anywhere."

With a horrified cry, the man stumbled away and began to run.

"Whoa, that was intense." Malik's voice came from behind him. "You are one scary mofo, sir. I m-mean Taviano."

Taviano turned to find the hole in the pavement filling with dirt and gravel. The fingers of one dead hand, rapidly vanishing, gave the only sign of what would lie concealed there. As Taviano watched, Malik finished his task and passed his hand horizontally over the ground. It smoothed, until only a few cracks indicated it had been a hole moments before.

"You have impressive control," Taviano said. He cocked his

head, studying Malik. The young vampire quivered but waited, still. "I have not seen a bloodbeast with power over the earth before. But that's a puzzle for later. I must find Paul."

"Where do we start?"

Taviano paused, surprised. "You wish to help me?"

"Well, sure," Malik said, as if it were obvious. "Paul is special."

"He is to me. But...how do you know that?"

Malik frowned. "Huh. How *do* I know that? He was nice, and he was willing to tackle three huge assholes to save a stranger. I think, though...it's more than that."

Taviano's demon was alert suddenly, but not aggressive. It radiated a sense of tension as Malik worked through his feelings.

"My passenger, or demon or whatever you want to call it. It wants me to help you. It—"

Malik crooked his head, eyes narrowing as he listened to his internal monster. Sudden surprise widened his eyes. "It recognized Paul!"

"Recognized how? As if it's seen him before?" Was that alarming or comforting? Taviano wasn't sure.

Malik slowly shook his head. "I don't think so. But something about Paul felt familiar."

Familiar. Like Paul had felt familiar to Taviano after mere moments together. Of course, in Taviano's case, Paul turned out to be a descendant of his boyhood lover.

He narrowed his eyes at Malik. "What do you know about the vampire who turned you?"

"Almost nothing, honest. I was still coming back. I guess. From being dead. I heard her say something, and then another vampire jumped her. I ran."

"The one who attacked, it wasn't Bronislav?"

"The dude from tonight? No. I would have guessed Chinese,

but it was so fast I didn't stick around for a good look."

This was important, Taviano sensed. Something about Malik, his connection to Paul. He needed to know.

"Will you try something with me? I'm not sure it will work. But"—Taviano gave an involuntary shake—"I don't know what else to do other than run all over Boston and hope Bronislav hasn't…" He couldn't even finish the thought.

"Uh, sure. Whatever you think."

Taviano looked around the alley and rejected it. Too easy for them to be disturbed. Revealing his lair was troubling, but he needed a quiet space.

"Follow me," he ordered, and took off at an easy run that sped up as Malik kept pace.

They leapt to the rooftops and reached the townhouse in less than a minute. Taviano bit back a moan as he remembered Paul dubbing it "Castle Dracula" on Christmas night. He guided Malik in through the door on the roof, to a sitting room on the third floor that Paul had recently refurnished.

A comfortable rug covered the wooden floor, with two over-stuffed chairs and a deep couch making a kind of den that faced the huge TV Paul had ordered. They often watched shows up there in the evening, before Taviano went out to hunt and ensure the safety of the North End.

Taviano knelt on the rug, heels beneath his seat, and gestured for Malik to do the same. "I've found when I absorb another bloodbeast that its memories come with it, even the echo of prior memories if the bloodbeast I've killed had itself consumed another."

Malik shivered. "Oh man, less talk about consuming, okay? It makes my guy nervous."

Taviano nodded. "Our demons seem to be in some kind of sync, at least over Paul. I want to see if I can guide yours through its memories and look for the connection."

"Creepy."

"Close your eyes, and think about breathing. I know you don't have to, but I want you to make the effort. Make your lungs fill. And empty. Good, like that. Let your eyes close. Don't think about anything but your breathing. Listen to the sound it makes as you draw in the air…" Taviano's voice trailed off as he let a tinge of his magic seep forward, toward the vampire kneeling across from him.

Malik breathed it in with his next inhalation. Taviano's magic followed that breath into Malik's airways, then lungs, and then into his ichor.

Damn, I'm late again, Malik thought as he crossed the square. Taviano recognized the buildings around Malik from pictures he'd seen—they were on the Harvard University campus in Cambridge. Obviously late at night, the only sounds were a wind rustling the trees and distant noises of traffic. Malik passed under an arch, and something grabbed him, then pulled him into deep shadows between two buildings.

"I'm sorry to do this so abruptly," a woman said, the dim light catching on her fangs. "The passenger in me says you are crucial. The circle must grow." And then she struck, draining Malik so quickly he barely had time to understand what was happening. She bit at her own wrist and held it to Malik's lips. He couldn't even move at first, but then he felt a trickle of something that was both cold and hot touch his tongue. It was the best thing he'd ever tasted and he began to drink more, swallowing greedily, sure he could never get enough.

The vampire eventually pushed his head away, but gently. "Enough, little one. I will help you through the next phase of your metamorphosis as best I can." She held Malik tightly but soothingly as his organs failed, singing to him softly as his heart slowed and the world dimmed. Malik's last thought as a mortal was, "I'm never going to finish my Geology paper in time." And then he was dead.

Until he wasn't. He opened his eyes to look up into the smiling face of a woman who appeared to be in her fifties. Although the shadows were still thick, he could see her clearly, including needle-sharp fangs in her smile.

"Welcome, little one. You did so well. Do you hear the song of your passenger yet?"

Malik wanted to ask what she meant, but suddenly he was aware of another presence in his brain, or maybe in his heart. Something that had a separate identity yet was inextricably bound up within him. It was excited, he could tell, although he heard no words and didn't know how he knew what it felt.

He nodded at the woman.

"Excellent. The quintessence is known. The circle must grow before it can be squared—"

That was all she had time for as a hand with nails long as claws grasped her shoulder and yanked her away. Malik glimpsed a slender man with dark hair, monolid eyes that flashed with fury, and yellowish pale skin. The new thing inside him flared with panic and fear as the two vampires—as they obviously were—tore at each other. The woman who'd attacked him fought hard, but the man seemed to be stronger.

"Run," she yelled to Malik, and the passenger in his soul agreed.

"You can't possibly think to win," the male snarled. "Too many of us have seen the truth. We are meant to rule."

Then she shrieked as the male vampire twisted her head viciously. Malik's passenger throbbed with sorrow and loss as she suffered, but he was already running running running, *faster than he would have ever imagined possible. He knew when the woman died, and felt the man coming after him.*

As if he were possessed, his left hand rose and his feet led him

straight toward a concrete wall. Before he knew what was happening,
he was sinking into the wall, its cool interior hiding him from
pursuit. He waited, terrified, for the murdering vampire to find him.
But eventually he realized that the wall must have hidden him well
enough. He was safe for the moment. But now what?

Taviano withdrew his magic as Malik forced out a breath. He
had learned nothing of a connection to Paul, but he let out a
shaky breath himself. He had seen both of those vampires before.
The woman he'd only glimpsed once and from a distance, as she
fed a drop of ichor to a group of humans and incited an orgy.
The male, though—he'd tried to help murder Paul at Christmas.
He was one that Taviano's demon had let live in order to spread
the word Taviano had claimed the North End.

Perhaps the attack on Malik's maker had nothing to do with
Paul. But when it came to these demons in vampires' bodies,
coincidence was rarely a factor. The bloodbeasts had a way of
pulling together events that only seemed random until one's
perspective shifted, and then suddenly disparate threads would
resolve into a tapestry.

"We're going to Cambridge," he announced, rising. Malik
stood as well. "Your maker was kind, something I've rarely seen
in any of us. I've no idea what she meant about a circle or the
quintessence, but let's find out what her murderer knows."

Grimly, he added, "Cambridge might become an open territory after tonight."

EIGHT

Paul

P AUL KICKED AT the steel door again, damaging only his toe. "Dammit."

He had no idea where the scary vampire had dragged him. They'd been running so fast—maybe even faster than Taviano could go—and between the wickedly strong hand clutching him around his ribs and the speed, he hadn't been able to get his breath. On the brink of passing out, he'd barely registered what was happening as the vampire darted into a big stone tower of some kind. Then the guy had carried Paul down a flight of stairs, chucked him into an empty concrete room, and slammed the door.

Only as his breath came back to him had Paul realized, with surprise, that he was alive. For some reason, the vampire hadn't drained him. So why had he been snatched up?

Only one answer occurred to him: He must be bait for Taviano.

The more he thought about it, the more certain he became. This bastard who'd yanked him from the alley must have been watching him. That was why he'd felt so creepy outside the North End earlier. Watched and waited for a time he could rush in, kidnap Paul, and get away before Taviano could react.

"Wait, that makes no sense," Paul said aloud, smacking his own head. "How would a vampire have been watching me during the day?"

On the other hand, Malik was apparently able to move around before Taviano would have even risen for the day. So maybe vampires had different sleep schedules, or different ways to tolerate some sun? Taviano was all Paul had to go by.

Problem for another time. For now, he had to see if there was a way out of this room before the scary fucker returned.

With ichor-jacked eyes and ears, Paul scanned the dim space. Concrete walls, a row of narrow windows set high, a bucket (*Ew! No way I'm using that*), a blanket, and some plastic bottles of water. The windows were about ten feet up and only a few inches high, probably there for ventilation. Even with his skinny ass, no way he'd be able to climb through, even if he could get up to them.

No furniture or other clue to what the room had been used for. From beyond the window, he could hear cars moving distantly, but not many. The rest of the building he was in sounded empty except for the scurrying of a few rats.

Ugh, rats. All God's creatures and so forth, but those naked tails freaked him out. At least he couldn't hear any in the cell with him.

Paul tugged the blanket into a seat against the wall opposite the steel door, and sat to assess. The room was chilly but not unbearable; still, he was grateful he had his jacket and the bastard hadn't ripped it. The water, blanket and bucket implied the vampire intended to keep him alive, at least for a little while. So, yay? The run through the streets was hazy, but he was pretty sure they hadn't been running long enough to leave Boston. That was good, too.

Taviano's demon was pretty badass. When Taviano didn't

fight it, the thing seemed capable of pretty huge tricks. So it wasn't just wishful thinking that it might be able to find him.

And then what? If he'd been taken as bait, probably the vampire who snatched him figured he could win a territory fight if Taviano were distracted by keeping Paul alive.

Then Paul's job was to not be a distraction, and to find a way to warn Taviano.

"Anytime now, brain," he said aloud. "This is a crisis. Give me a brilliant plan like tying a note to one of those disgusting rats and Disney-princessing it to go find my boo."

A low, feminine chuckle came from above his head, and Paul leapt away like a shot, scrabbling on hands and knees across the floor. He fell back on his ass, hands behind him on cold concrete, and scanned the shadows frantically.

Movement from above made his heart pound. Into the small shaft of light from the inset windows, something moved along the wall. It became a woman, crawling along like a lizard until she was fully visible. Even in the dimness, Paul could make out pale skin, dark hair pulled back into some kind of ponytail, and shining eyes.

But he couldn't *feel* her. The ichor in his body was quiet, for all the world as if he were alone.

The woman smiled; light from the windows sparkled on her fangs, ending any hope she was something other than a vampire. But she wasn't the one who'd dragged him here.

"Do you feel like a princess? Perhaps one captured and thrown in a tower, awaiting rescue from her knight?" she asked, in a voice that was melodious and surprisingly deep for a woman. Her accent was European, in a way that made him think of the Greek owner of the diner where he used to work.

Paul forced himself to his feet and set his jaw. "First off, if I want to present as a woman, it's nobody's business but mine. I don't, but you didn't know that so it's just rude. Second, that wall-sticking shit is creepy."

Still smiling, the woman turned and climbed head-first to the floor, then slithered forward until she lay splayed facedown. Paul took a few more steps back until his ass hit the steel door.

Between one blink and the next, the woman was on her bare feet, head crooked as she studied him with an intense, possessive gaze. He returned the favor. Her outfit was tight, red-striped athletic pants and a zippered top with long sleeves, in royal blue.

"Did you steal that combo from lululemon's trash bin?" Paul asked. "Interesting fashion choice."

The woman didn't answer but came closer. She was petite, probably no more than five-one, but Paul knew that meant nothing. She'd be able to tear him apart.

Inches away, she peered up at him, burning eyes roaming over his face and body. Thankfully not lingering on his neck, but still, he was starting to feel a little objectified even before her gaze centered on his crotch.

"Hey, not cool. My eyes are up here, Thumbelina."

She released another throaty chuckle. "You're wondering why you can't feel me." It wasn't a question, but Paul nodded. "Because I didn't want you to. Until now."

A wave of *something* hit Paul, driving him to his knees. The ichor in him was churning so hard he thought he might be sick. He'd swear there was no sound in the room, but whatever was coming from the woman pulsed and burned in his head like an Eighties acid rock band.

Abruptly it stopped and he looked up at her from his new position.

"That's better," she purred over him. "I wondered how the kalesménos psychí would react to you. If it would feel the urge to flee or fight or cower. Apparently not."

"The call-us-what now?"

"My soul guest. I thought, somehow, this moment would be more dramatic."

"It's plenty dramatic for me, thanks," Paul muttered. "Sorry to disappoint."

"I suspect Bronislav was correct after all. The quintessence is diluted by time."

The name triggered a rush of memories, of Taviano, on that first night, telling him how he'd been changed by a vampire named—

"Bronislav! The dickhead that made Taviano."

She ignored that. "It's fortunate the child Taviano is so weak. He never realized what he had."

"So what is this? You're using me as a lure to trap Taviano? Because let me tell you, that didn't go so well for the last bunch of vamps that tried to use me to challenge him."

The vampire reached out a pale hand and ran it through Paul's hair. He cringed at the touch and her smile grew. She tightened her fingers until the pull on his hair became painful.

"And what would I want with your Taviano?"

"Uh, his territory?" Paul guessed.

She laughed and brought her face closer to his. A mixture of spicy scents, some kind of oil on her hair, and old, dried blood wafted at Paul. He choked.

"Listerine. It's your friend," he said, gagging.

"I used to play those games of territory, it's true." She released his hair and turned away. "For hundreds of years. But then I learned that the true game is so much bigger."

She reached the wall and slithered up it into the shadows again. This time Paul could see that she used her fingernails and toes to grip, her power and strength making the climb look effortless.

"Hey, these water bottles?" Paul called after her. "Not cool for the environment."

A final low laugh came from the shadows, and then silence.

Paul sank back down against the wall. "Well, that was ominous. And cryptic. She's a cryptic cryptid. Hey, that'd be a great name for a band."

Fuck. He really needed to find a way to warn Taviano.

NINE

Taviano

TAVIANO LEAPT TO the top of a mid-rise apartment building and waited for Malik. He wanted to move faster, but the young vampire wasn't yet powerful enough. For hours, though, Malik did his best, using fingers wedged between bricks to crawl up surfaces when he couldn't jump.

Taviano was in a misery of contradictions. He wanted to root out every possible hiding place for the vampire who claimed the Cambridge territory. He wanted to understand why his blood-beast tolerated the presence of Malik and, indeed, seemed to believe the boy was important.

Why was Bronislav back, and why now?

And where was his Paul?

He moaned aloud, scanning the horizon left and right as Malik reached the rooftop. They'd covered much of Cambridge and he didn't know where else to look. If the vampire here had a lair like Taviano's, it might be concealed in something so ordinary they'd never find it.

"Mr. Taviano sir?"

"Yes, Malik?"

"I'm slowing you down. Do you want—I mean, would it be easier if you left me behind?"

Malik's voice trembled. Taviano understood. He'd spent many, many years alone, once he'd escaped from Bronislav. He'd had questions and few answers, but mostly he'd been lonely. Malik had just as many questions and fears.

"I won't leave you," Taviano vowed. "But let's try something." Cautiously, he stepped closer to Malik, feeling for his demon's reaction. The boy's eyes were wide but he remained still as Taviano approached. They were feet apart, then inches, and still his demon felt calm.

"All right?" he asked.

Malik seemed to understand his question and returned a short nod.

"Good. I want to carry you. We'll be able to cover more of the territory, and you won't need to draw on your bloodbeast's power as much. I imagine you're beginning to feel hunger pains as it is."

Malik swallowed. "I am. I thought, because it fed off that mugger in the alley, that it would be satisfied but…" He looked down at his stomach. "It's practically gnawing at me."

"You've called on quite a bit of magic tonight, between the grave and following me. Have you learned yet that you need not drain a human to the point of death?"

"I-I don't have much control, sir. When my passenger takes over, it does what it wants."

"First lesson then. You are in control."

"It doesn't feel like it."

"The same way you've taught yourself to draw on only a little magic to manipulate the earth—that's the key. Your bloodbeast *wants* things, I know. But if you stay strong, you can keep it from taking over your will."

He listened to the night, and in moments heard familiar sounds—the rapid click of heeled shoes on cement, the scuff of leather behind. He opened an arm, and when Malik stepped close, he wrapped the boy up and leapt to the street below, just feet behind his potential prey.

A young woman walked alone, hands stuffed in her coat pockets, and a man in a bomber jacket followed her. He didn't seem to be on his guard, though. Taviano followed the pair for a block to be sure, but the man made no effort to catch up to the woman.

It seemed nothing more than two people passing along the same street. Almost disappointed, Taviano began to turn away when his attention was dragged back. The young woman had stumbled and fallen to her knees. The man rushed over to her, and Taviano tensed.

"Are you okay? Did you hurt yourself?" the man asked, hands reaching out to help the woman up. Distracted, he didn't notice a second woman emerge from an alley, a pistol held low and close to her side.

Just when the man was engaged in helping up the one who tripped, the armed woman stepped to his back, pressed the barrel of the pistol to his shirt, and snarled, "Give me your fucking wallet and your phone."

The man stiffened in alarm and the woman he'd been trying to help pushed him away. "Took you long enough," she said scornfully to the one with a gun. She reached out toward the man, curling her fingers in a gesture for him to surrender his belongings.

With trembling hands, he reached into his back pocket and eased out his wallet. The woman he'd been trying to help snatched it from him and began to rifle through it, while the second reached for his watch.

"Control," Taviano whispered to Malik. "Visualize your bloodbeast forced into a cage or a container of some kind."

Calling on his powers, he made a wind whistle toward the tableau on the sidewalk, stirring up trash into a confusing swirl. The two muggers flinched as torn paper and plastic bags covered their faces momentarily. "You take the one with the wallet into that alley. I'll be right behind you."

As Malik obeyed, Taviano rushed at the one with the pistol. With a hand on her waist, and the other holding up the woman's gun hand by the wrist, he pulled her into the shadowed alley. Malik appeared next to him, arms wrapped tightly around the woman who'd acted as bait.

Before either woman could scream, Taviano plunged his fangs into one neck and sensed Malik do the same. Hot blood poured over his tongue from the puncture wounds he made with needle-sharp canine teeth, and he lapped it up eagerly. After a few moments of bliss, though, he stopped drinking. He lifted his head and saw that Malik was still at the neck of his victim.

"That's enough," he said, putting a hand on the boy's shoulder and felt him tense, heard him growl low in his throat. "You've taken all you need to satisfy your bloodbeast. Remember that you are in control and then… Make. It. Stop!"

At first, he wasn't sure Malik could or would listen to him, and he prepared to separate vampire from food source. But then the boy straightened up. With a gasp, he pulled his head back and away from the woman in his arms.

Malik blinked uncertainly, his eyes narrowing to focus on the trickle of blood still running down her neck. His jaw muscles clenched and brow furrowed.

"Good work," Taviano said. He knew the struggle Malik was experiencing, the desire to take it all, regardless of what the demon actually needed. "Now we heal the wound, like this." He nipped at the end of a finger, then smeared his ichor on the wounds of the victim he held. The puncture wounds closed immediately, and Malik copied him.

"Is this when we make them forget, sir?" Malik asked, his voice sounding strained from wrestling with his bloodbeast.

"Exactly, and sometimes an order. I try to impose a penance on such miscreants as these, to force them to make some atonement. Like this."

Fixing his gaze on the woman he held, Taviano released a stream of his magic into her. "Why do you do this? Hunt people like you are jackals?"

In a sleepy voice, the woman said, "These yuppie farts think they're better 'n us. They ain't. It's a kick seeing how scared we can make 'em."

"Then fear is your punishment. You are terrified of the dark. Even of deep shadows. Things are waiting for you there, with fang and claw. Until you gather the same amount of money you have stolen and donate it to a charity, you will never know a moment's peace in darkness."

He nodded to Malik. "You try."

Malik nodded, then mimicked what Taviano had done. He'd just finished speaking to his victim when the man they'd mugged shouted from behind them. They whirled to find him standing in the alley entrance. "What the hell are you doing?"

Malik panicked at the intrusion, and Taviano felt a flare of power surge from the young vampire. Dirt and pebbles began to bounce on the ground, building up with the youth's anxiety. Malik's bloodbeast was surging, ready to take control if he faltered.

Taviano rushed to the man and hypnotized him, telling him to pick up his wallet and watch, then forget all that had happened in the last ten minutes. He turned back to find Malik so agitated his eyes had taken on a red spark. His bloodbeast was fighting to take advantage of the distraction. Without thinking about it,

Taviano let out his own magic and sent a warm cocoon of air to soothe and comfort Malik.

He was utterly unprepared for what happened next. As the edge of his magicked air met Malik's trembling earth, he felt their bloodbeasts connect. *Something* unseen rippled back and forth between Taviano and Malik, something powerful.

Time stood still in the alley. Taviano couldn't have moved if he wanted to. Whatever this effect was, stretched between him and the boy vampire, it felt more magical than anything he released on his own. Yet there was a sense of incompleteness to it, as well.

This formless magic between them needed… *What* did it need? Direction? A key? He could almost feel the lack at the edge of his consciousness. It had a shape to it, or more like a hollow. He had no idea what would fit into the hollow.

The pebbles plinked as they dropped back to the ground, and Taviano's wind died away completely. Whatever the magic had formed, it was apparently unstable. The alley became completely still except for the mesmerized breathing of the two female muggers.

"What *was* that?"

"To be honest, Malik, I don't know."

Shaking his head, Taviano risked drawing a bit of power to send the females away to their punishment, then made sure the man they had mugged was moving to safety.

He needed to continue the search, but whatever had happened between him and Malik was important.

TEN

Paul

WHAT WAS PAUL going to do? There was no doubt in his mind that Taviano would find him. But this—this *thing* in the hideous track suit would be waiting. She was obviously powerful if tasteless, maybe even more powerful than his boo.

"Sorry, babe," he whispered into the darkness, feeling bad for his doubts. Taviano would shank this skinny bitch, or whatever he had to do to keep Paul safe.

It was Paul that was the problem, of course. This was twice now that he'd been grabbed. The first time it had been a way to lure Taviano. This time...well, it wasn't so clear what Vampirella wanted. Her words indicated something other than a turf war was going on, but if so, what the hell did it have to do with Paul?

The word she used—quintessence. It seemed familiar, but he couldn't remember from where. It meant the best, didn't it, or something like that? He thought so, anyway.

He peed in the bucket, wincing at the odor that filled his cell. "Of course I had asparagus for lunch. Gross." Well, when Vampirella or Bratislava came back, hopefully it would totally nauseate their hyped-up senses.

Cracking open one of the irresponsibly small bottles of water, Paul paced the inside of his cell. He kept looking up at the line of small windows. Worth a try to wiggle his ass through, but he had no way to get up there.

Maybe the ichor left in his body would help. Setting aside his bottle, he approached the wall directly under the bank of windows. He crooked his fingers like he'd seen the Mistress of the Snark do and tried to climb. Immediate fail, and on top of that, he tore off the nail on his index finger.

"Son of a bitch," he moaned, sucking on the slightly bloodied digit. "No wonder Lois Lane hated getting captured. Being a liability sucks."

If Taviano made him a vampire, it would solve at least one situation. To be honest, though, Paul wasn't sure if he really wanted that. The ninja skills and assorted superpowers would be pretty sweet. Plus, he and Taviano could really get down and dirty without worrying about a pesky bone breaking or something.

Drinking blood, though…Paul shuddered. He supposed if he had a beast or a demon or what-the-fuck-ever sharing his body, that wouldn't really be a problem anymore. He could get behind Taviano's mission of only feeding on the bad guys, and using his powers to try to help. But what if he slipped and killed someone? Paul wasn't sure how he'd deal with that. Taviano was plenty tortured about the harm he'd done before he knew what was going on, or when he wasn't fully in control.

Yet what was the alternative to turning? Aging while Taviano stayed the same. He was already twenty-five to Taviano's twenty-two-year-old body. In no time at all, Paul would be a silver fox, and Taviano would look the same. And then worst of all, imagine how Taviano would feel when Paul simply died of old age. Given his family's longevity, they might have sixty, seventy years, but after that? Taviano wasn't exactly a social creature. He'd love and care for Paul through his death, and then back to centuries of wandering unless he happened to meet someone else. Someone who saw the goodness inside Taviano and knew that his only job in the world was to help Taviano see the same about himself.

A pang of jealousy stabbed at Paul. Even understanding that immortality meant Taviano would get the shitty end of the deal on "til death do us part", Paul hated the idea of someone else loving Taviano the way that he did. Selfish? Sure. But it didn't signify. Taviano and Paul belonged together. That was why Taviano's demon had worked events to bring them together, right? Because they were fated mates or something.

Weren't they?

For the first time, doubt crept in. Not of Taviano, of course. Never that. But the demon inside? Who knew, really, why it had pulled Taviano to Paul's side. The creepy female had something in mind to do with Paul, too, and he was pretty sure it wasn't bumping uglies.

Another shudder. Bisexuality was real, but he so wasn't that. Even that gigantic Bronislav did nothing for Paul. No, he was apparently a ten on the Taviano-sexual scale.

Which was why it sucked he was a hostage again.

On and on his thoughts cycled as hours seemed to tick by. Worrying about being a liability, considering and rejecting the idea of going vamp, sorrowing over what that would mean for Taviano and eternity.

Ugh. This was why he kept busy, so the noise in his head would stay under control.

He was on perhaps his three *thousandth* pass around the cell when something finally happened. A noise was coming from beyond the door, some kind of disturbance. Maybe Taviano had found him? Maybe there was a fight?

He pressed his ear against the door, straining to hear. A couple of voices, he thought. No sound of fighting. That was good, maybe everyone was talking the situation through, like mature bloodsuckers.

Hah, fat chance. The way these demons got around each other, a war was far more likely.

The voices were coming closer. Now Paul could make out a high, feminine voice, and a rumble that sounded like the noises from Bronislav when he'd dragged Paul in here.

He pressed himself back against the wall opposite the door. He had no stupid illusions he could throw himself on Bronislav and get out of there, so his best option was to hang back and try to see what was going on.

The door swung open with a boom that echoed through the cavernous building beyond. Although the ichor in his body was almost spent, enough remained that Paul could see Bronislav's dark mass filling the doorway. He had two people in his grip, and he pushed them into the room.

"Company for you," he snarled, burning eyes fixed on Paul's.

Talk about fight-or-flight. Paul wanted nothing more than to be far FAR away from that scary-ass vampire. So fixed was he on Bronislav that it wasn't until the vampire pulled the door shut that he recognized the other two cellmates.

"Paulie?" asked Nonna. "Is that you?"

And then he heard a harsh male voice, "Paul Leo Alligood. What in the name of God have you gotten your grandmother and me mixed up in?"

Sigh.

"Hi, Dad."

ELEVEN

Paul

H IS FATHER COULD wait. Paul rushed to Nonna's side. "Are you all right? Did that shithead do anything to you?"

Nonna had on some pajamas under her housecoat, and fluffy slippers on her feet. Paul slipped off his jacket and put it around her shoulders. His father was dressed in a sweater and chinos, which Paul figured would keep him warm enough.

"I-I don't know," Nonna answered as she clutched at the sides of Paul's jacket around her. "I have the strangest feeling I've been dreaming."

"Is this some homosexual hazing ritual?" his father demanded. "Are you involved in one of those CDMS clubs?"

"It's BDSM, Gianni," Nonna said before Paul could respond. "Read a book some time."

"Ma—"

"Don't 'Ma' me. I thought I raised you better than this. Jumping to homophobic conclusions. Of course this has nothing to do with Paulie being gay." She turned to Paul and leaned in close so only he could hear. "You said Taviano isn't famiglia. Are you sure about that?"

Paul shook his head. "No mob stuff. I don't know what it's about, to be honest. But..." He looked back and forth from his father to his grandmother. "It doesn't seem to be about Taviano either."

"Who's Taviano? What are we doing here? Your mother will be sick with worry."

"Gianni, enough," Nonna snapped. "Taviano is Paulie's ragazzo, a lovely boy and he treats Paulie like a prince."

"I can't believe you've been associating with this, this—"

"Dad, shut the hell up," Paul barked. "You can give me the bullshit 'no son of mine' speech later. We've got to get out of here first. I don't even know where we are."

"Cambridge," Gianni said. "What? I don't know how I got here but I saw the sign to Harvard Square right before we, uh, got into this place..." His voice trailed off into uncertainty as he looked around the cell.

"Tell me what happened to you," Paul said. "Maybe there's a hint there."

Nonna shrugged. "My door buzzer rang. I figured it was Mr. Marsden next door, forgot his keys again, so I buzzed the front door open."

Paul groaned. "Nonna! I begged you to be more careful."

"Yeah, yeah. A few seconds later there was a knock. When I answered, that huge man was standing in the hallway. He had a package in his hand and he said he was having trouble reading the label. I told him to come in while I got my reading glasses and then—"

"Everything went fuzzy," Gianni finished. "The same thing happened to me."

"You invited him in," Paul said, nodding slowly. "So the barrier whatsit dropped and he could whammy you."

"You know about this," Nonna said accusingly. "That man—something about him reminds me of Taviano. You say it's not mob, I believe you. But Paulie, you have to tell me. What's going on?"

Paul sighed. "You're going to think I'm batshit, but okay." He took a deep breath and let it out on a sigh. "So, it turns out vampires are real. Undead, blood-sucking, hate the sun, all of that. Except garlic is fine, and crosses don't affect them. And that's what this guy is. He's a vampire named Bronislav. What he wants with us, I don't know."

Gianni sputtered. "What a load of bullcrap. You expect me to believe—"

"Stai zitto," Nonna said. Gianni snorted but shut up like his mother ordered. She peered at Paul, her blue eyes picking up the little light from the windows. They shone at him shrewdly. "Your Taviano. He's a vampire, too?"

Paul could only nod.

"Well, that explains how he eats so many cannoli and keeps that sexy body."

"Nonna!"

She shrugged. "I can't look at my grandson's boyfriend and think he's handsome?"

"He's gorgeous but that's not the point. Last Christmas, when I got mugged, Taviano saved me. He told me what he was but he planned to make my memories go away, like it was all a dream. They can do that, so I guess that's how Bronislav got you here. By the end of the night, I begged him not to make me forget. Then some other vamps attacked us, I got killed—"

"WHAT!"

"I got better, obvs. Vampires can heal things with their blood. Taviano used it on me." Paul shrugged, not about to explain exactly how he'd gotten ichor into his body. "Anyway, there was a big-ass fight, Taviano kicked the shit out of the bad vamps, and now he runs the North End of Boston."

"Mafia," Gianni snorted. "Of course my homo son would

end up with a mobster."

"It isn't the mafia! Jesus Christ!" Paul ran his hands through his hair. "Look, vampires have territories, right? And Taviano keeps the North End free of other vampires who break into his territory. The job came with the mansion and lots of money; Taviano didn't get all that by killing. He goes out at night and does what he can to stop bad things from happening even with ordinary people."

"So he's, what was that movie you made me watch? Batman? You have a vampiro ragazzo who's Batman?" Nonna sounded more amused than annoyed.

"What mansion?" Gianni asked.

"Of course that's what you'd focus on. Yes, Dad, my boyfriend has a mansion and a shit-ton of money."

"Still sounds like mob to me," he sniffed.

"There's, uh, something else. Something weird."

"Weirder than being kidnapped from my apartment in the middle of the night and brought to a mysterious building with my son and grandson? I'm all ears."

"Um, Taviano knew your grandfather, back in Italy. Calogero was his, uh, friend when they were boys."

He expected surprise, or a gasp, or even a laugh, in a can-this-story-get-any-stranger way. What he didn't expect was for his grandmother to rise to her full five-foot-two height and snap, "Is he Taviano *Adelfio?*"

"Well, uh, yes."

"I can't believe it. Paulie, if you knew how he hurt my grandfather, you'd have nothing to do with him."

Paul started to protest, but the door screeched as it was flung open, this time by a vampire Paul vaguely recognized. He had Chinese features, tight-fitting fashionable clothes, and blindingly white fangs that glinted as he smiled. The vampire threw two more people into the cell. "Now it's a party," he said, laughing as he slammed the cell closed again.

Two of Paul's cousins looked up from where they'd landed on their hands and knees. Both fortunately seemed to have been wearing moderately warm clothes when they were grabbed.

"Sofia! Luca!" Nonna exclaimed. "Are you babies all right?"

"Aunt Conchetta and Uncle Gianni?" Sofia was first on her feet, confused but with no obvious injuries. "And Paul, too? What the hell is going on?"

"Vampires," Gianni said disgustedly. "My son says he's shacking up with a mobster vampire and we're being targeted in some kind of family revenge move."

"That isn't at all what I said," Paul protested, helping Luca up.

"Vampires, huh?" Luca said, sounding a little dazed. Probably still feeling the whammy. "Cool."

"Right?"

"Wait," Sofia interjected. "Is that bell'uomo with the huge mansion a vampire?"

"Yeah," Paul said, "Fangs and everything."

"Does everybody know this…this *monster* committing mortal sins with Paul?"

"Dad, I swear to God—"

"Tell me about the sex. Right now," Sofia demanded. Gianni gagged, and Nonna shushed them all.

"Basta!" she shouted. "Giggle later. Paulie, before this room gets any more crowded with our family, tell me what you know. What does this have to do with Calogero? No, hush," she said, pointing a finger at Luca who was about to ask a question. "Paulie."

Paul tried to explain what he knew, about the bloodbeasts sharing the body with a vampire, about how Taviano's demon implied he'd brought Taviano to Boston specifically to find Paul, how Taviano had fought and won to keep Paul safe, and how he'd spent the past year protecting the North End.

"I saw three stronzi cleaning graffiti off a wall the other day," Sofia muttered, daring the evil eye from Nonna. "Thought that was strange but now it makes sense."

"Anyway, everything's been quiet for a while. Then tonight, we got rounded up by these two vamps, and there's a third one, way scarier. She said something..." Paul closed his eyes, trying to remember. *C'mon, brain. Work!*

"She said something like, the quintessence is diluted. Quint means five, doesn't it?" he asked Nonna.

She nodded. "Quintessence. That's out of old myths and legends about alchemists. Some people used to believe that there were four elements: Earth, air, fire and water. The quintessence was what alchemists called the fifth element, which they thought made up heavenly bodies, like the Sun and the stars."

"Taviano does shit with air and fire," Paul mused.

"What kind of shit?" Sofia asked.

"Oh, he can call up a wind strong enough to throw someone, or make air get warm around me when it's cold. He doesn't use the fire thing much, but I've seen him light the fireplace from across the room. And the chick he killed used it in the fight to make his clothes burn."

"Your life is amazing," Luca sighed.

"Nonna, when you taught Literature, was there anything connecting the elements and vampires?"

She shook her head. "No, nothing I can recall. The Greeks had legends about blood drinkers like Lamia and stirges, but they weren't what we'd consider vampires. Or at least, what you're telling us Taviano is like."

A low, derisive chuckle drifted down from the shadows, and

all five humans froze. As one, they looked up. Paul fought the urge to shriek when he met the female vampire's glittering eyes, peering from a corner of the ceiling.

"Legends. Myths." Another chuckle. "Even now, it amazes me what stories survive and which are forgotten. Which mutate into entirely new forms, so only those who've lived long enough can recognize the kernel and whence it came." She crept down the wall head first again, and Luca did scream.

Paul pushed the others behind him and faced the descending vampire. "Is this it, Vampirella? Or are you bringing more of my family so we can all watch when Taviano eats you?"

She ignored the bravado but stretched out one clawed hand, still holding on to the wall with the other. She passed it over the heads of Paul's assembled family, and nodded. "Yes, Bronislav's intuition was correct. You collectively possess enough of the quintessence for the ritual. Just one more piece to locate, and we can begin. Sleep well, children. I'll see you soon."

With that, she climbed backwards up into the shadows once more.

"Cryptic much?" Luca muttered.

"I called her the cryptic cryptid in my head," Paul agreed.

"That'd be a great name for a band," Sofia added.

"You're all idiots," Gianni said.

TWELVE

Taviano

TWO HOURS OF searching, and Taviano was near despair. Even carrying Malik, he'd only been able to accomplish a superficial search of Cambridge. And of course he couldn't even be sure Paul was *in* Cambridge.

Or alive.

No, stop that, he ordered himself. One absolute belief he held was that his demon would know if Paul died. It also knew that it would have to fight every day thereafter to keep Taviano from ending his own existence by walking into the sun. Or maybe Paul's fate was tied to its own agenda. Either way, his demon radiated unease, concern, but not despair.

In so many ways, this was what Taviano had feared since Christmas Eve, when vampires had tried to kill Paul and drive Taviano out of the North End. The darkness of his supernatural life always threatened to extinguish Paul's light.

Perhaps he'd been fooling himself for the past year. Giving money to support Paul's causes, helping Paul make a safe and comfortable home, even guarding the North End from monsters both human and inhuman, had all felt transitory. Unsustainable. Unless Paul really wanted to become a vampire—and the bloodbeast agreed to turn him—time would eventually separate them, even if Paul did not come to his senses earlier and leave of his own accord.

"A better man would have freed Paul long before this," Taviano whispered to himself.

"What do you mean?" Malik asked.

Taviano shook his head. "Forgive me, I'm rambling." He carried Malik to the roof of a convenient building and released him. They stood side by side, scanning the nighttime vista of Cambridge. "The truth is, I don't know where to look next."

"Would it—is it possible some of the other vampires might help us?"

Taviano frowned down at the boy. "What other vampires?"

"Well, there's the woman in the South End. Maybe not her, though. Her kills are sort of brutal. But the other lady, the one in the Dorchester neighborhood. I think she tries to choose her victims like Paul said you do."

"Why do you say that?"

"I've been hiding a lot, like I told you. But if I found another vampire, I'd get as close as my passenger told me was safe, to watch and see what I could learn. The Dorchester lady is the one I heard warn another vampire about you, in the North End."

Taviano considered. His experience when encountering another vampire had almost always been a case of fight-or-flee. The way their bloodbeasts reacted to one another was violent and chaotic.

Of course, the reaction between his demon and Malik's was different. Perhaps there were other vampires with whom he could also interact without violence?

"I have no other ideas. Can you guide us to the approximate location of this vampire?"

Malik gulped. "I can try. At least, I think I can show you where I was when I saw her."

Fifteen minutes later, Taviano followed Malik through a low stone wall with a sign declaring it the entrance to Dorchester Park. They moved silently along a paved pathway that led into the night-dark forest of beech and oak. Lamps revealed well-kept landscaping and signs of a beloved local park: A little house for book exchanges, benches in good repair, and a playground with equipment that looked new. The rhythmic sound of running feet told Taviano that joggers were unafraid, even at the current late hour.

"Are you sure this is where you saw her?" he asked Malik. "It seems an unlikely place for a vampire to haunt."

"I didn't see her kill anyone. I just saw her talking to another vampire. They were about"—Malik looked around and pointed to a fountain—"right there."

Taviano stood by the concrete basin, its jets turned off, probably due to the time of night. A few fallen leaves drifted in the still water of the fountain, and more lay along the path. He drew forth a little of his demon's magic. The dry leaves rose and began to swirl around in a spiral. It was the best way he could think to announce his presence and, hopefully, draw the Dorchester vampire to them.

"That's beautiful," Malik said, wide eyes on the dancing leaves. He stretched out a hand, laughing softly as Taviano's breeze tickled his skin.

Taviano let a little more magic out until the breeze grew in strength, rustling the trees around the fountain, shaking loose more leaves.

"Malik, hide. Right now," he ordered suddenly.

The boy flashed an alarmed look at him but didn't argue. He dove into the still fountain and kept going until he'd vanished into the basin itself.

Taviano turned slowly as he fought the screaming blend of

alertness and warning his bloodbeast was sending. At the edge of the plaza where the fountain stood, just in shadow, he felt the presence of a vampire.

"I mean no harm or conflict," he said, just loud enough for preternatural ears to hear. "I will not challenge you. I only hope to talk."

After a moment, the vampire moved forward, just inside a penumbra of shadow. Taviano let his wind die away, and waited cautiously as the leaves rustled to the ground.

"You're the North End," the vampire said, and took another step closer. Now Taviano could see it was a woman, possibly in her thirties when she died. Her large, almond-shaped eyes were dark, and black hair and brows suggested Indian heritage. Incongruously, she wore a long white coat, open over a modern blouse and pair of trousers.

"I am Taviano," he said, with a slight bow. "May we talk?"

The bloodbeast inside him was tense, but so far not aggressive or panicked. Through it, Taviano sensed a probing or testing coming from the woman. He remained still to let her see he was not there to fight.

A few moments later, the tendril of power was withdrawn. The vampire stepped fully into the light, though she remained at sufficient distance to flee.

"Doctor Rani Iqbal," the woman said. "Or Dorchester, if you prefer the custom of going by the name of our territory."

"Doctor?" Taviano couldn't hide his surprise.

"Yes. I work at the hospital complex nearby."

"I...see."

"Do you?" Dorchester edged closer. "Humans are precious to me. I will not permit you to harm anyone in my territory. You are possibly stronger but I am not easily defeated."

The water in the fountain roiled and began to swirl, much as the leaves Taviano had used earlier in a bid to draw this vampire's attention. A column of water rose and teetered, ready for Dorchester to send at Taviano if a fight should erupt.

"I promise you, Doctor Iqbal, that I come here with no intention to harm, but to ask for your help."

Dorchester cocked her head, then nodded abruptly. The tower of water splashed back down into the fountain and the surface quickly grew still again.

"Is this about the queen?"

Taviano frowned. "What queen?"

"Interesting. You don't know about Keres?"

"I don't believe I've ever heard that name."

"Perhaps you should get out of the North End more. Come, let's walk. As long as I'm away from my hospital rounds, I might as well ensure the park remains safe." She gestured peremptorily for Taviano to follow her. "You too, child," she said in a louder voice, tossed over her shoulder in the direction of the fountain.

"Malik, please join us," Taviano said. The boy emerged from the side of the basin, as simply as Taviano would walk under a waterfall, and leaving as little trace. Malik moved quickly to Taviano's side as they began to follow Dorchester. She gestured for them to catch up.

"Keres is one of the oldest vampires. In fact, she claims to be from the first brood. That assertion—which remains unproven, so far as I am aware—is the basis for her claim to be queen of us all."

"How have I never heard of her?"

Dorchester favored Taviano with a skeptical glance. "Maybe you should spend more time understanding our kind before you slaughter them."

"I don't slaughter," Taviano protested. "I never even claimed a territory before Christmas, and I only did so then when the vampire of the North End attacked my, my—"

"Your familiar. Or boyfriend. Whichever you prefer."

"You know about Paul?"

"Is that his name? I only know your reputation, that you murdered ten vampires who threatened your human."

"That's not true. I did kill two vampires, yes, but only after they attacked me and tried to murder Paul. I let two others go that same night. And since, I've been able to drive away all but one of the vampires who challenged me for my territory."

"And that one, you killed." It wasn't a question, but Taviano nodded.

"Reluctantly."

"Hm." Dorchester silently led the way along the path for a few minutes. Taviano felt her attention on the noises of the park around them. All seemed well, and finally she said, "Keres nominally claims the territory of Florence in what I understand is your homeland. However, as I said, she also claims queendom over all of our territories."

"Florence. That's one of the few cities in Europe where my maker never took me. After I freed myself from him and determined that my own family and friends were gone, I left Italy and never returned."

"Just as well," Dorchester said. "Keres is known for her capriciousness. You might have ended up her slave or have simply been absorbed by her blood spirit."

"Blood spirit. I've never heard it called that."

"My maker called it the passenger," Malik interjected.

"Passenger. Demon. Spirit. Bloodbeast. I've heard many terms over the years." Dorchester shook her head. "The truth is, none of us knows what this thing animating our bodies really is. Or what it wants."

"Besides blood."

Dorchester looked at Malik and gave a slight smile. "Yes, besides blood."

"You said this queen, Keres, is here? In America, do you mean?"

"No, I mean in Boston. She seems to share a trick I can do where my blood spirit can't sense her, but I actually saw her in the company of two other vampires, Cambridge and a big, dark-haired one I didn't know."

"Where did you see her?" Taviano demanded. "My Paul was taken tonight, I believe by my maker. Possibly that's who you saw in the company of the one who claims Cambridge. Malik and I have been searching for hours, but so far it's been fruitless. If you can show us where—"

"I will not go anywhere near that pack," Dorchester said firmly. "For more than thirty years, I've kept this neighborhood safe and I've avoided trouble with our kind. Luckily, most vampires in search of a territory are drawn to the more populous areas of Boston, so I've only had to fight a handful of times." She grinned, showing her fangs. "Make no mistake, though. I won those battles."

"And you're a doctor, too?" Malik asked. "How does that work?"

Dorchester gave a snort. "I worked hard for my medical degree and accreditations. I was in my first year of practice after completing my residency when my maker turned me. I wasn't about to let all that education go to waste. Once I learned how to accommodate my blood spirit's needs, I felt confident I was no danger to humans. At least, not to innocent humans who don't prey on others. It took some doing, but I became affiliated with a hospital and work the graveyard shift."

"For thirty years? Hasn't someone noticed you don't age?" Taviano asked, fascinated. The idea of integrating himself into the human world had never before occurred to him. It was an alluring dream.

"Yes, I've done the old trick of going away for a while and coming back under a different name. It's tricky, but once I let the hospital administrator in on my, well, special needs and qualifications, she was willing to help me."

"You told a human what you are?"

"Just as you did," Dorchester said sharply. "Belinda isn't my lover, the way your Paul apparently is, but she is my familiar. I protect and provide for her and her family; she facilitates my medical practice and handles the daylight tasks that are difficult for me."

"I want a familiar," Malik mumbled.

Dorchester smiled at him, kindly. "You're very young, both in actual years and in your undead state. Give it time, learn how best to use your gifts, and your spirit will help you forge a meaningful existence."

"Cool."

Taviano interrupted. "I respect that you don't wish to become involved directly, but if you could at least tell me where...?"

Dorchester stopped and turned to contemplate Taviano for a moment. "Malik, is it? Could you do me a small favor? I hear a drunken street fight beginning about four blocks in that direction. Would you be so kind as to break it up—gently—and send the clowns home? Not in their own cars, of course."

Malik looked between Taviano and Dorchester, then nodded. "Will do," he said, and sped away.

Once the boy was out of sight, Dorchester turned to Taviano and addressed him seriously. "I understand your anxiety over your familiar. But it would be suicide for you to challenge Keres, even if she weren't accompanied by two other vampires. And Malik would fare worse."

"I can't walk away from Paul," Taviano said firmly. "Malik need not accompany me. Perhaps you'd even consent to guide him. But Paul...he's all I have. The only person who matters to me. He has given so much of his light this past year, and I will not leave him. Not if there is any chance I can save him."

Dorchester sighed. "All right. I'll offer Malik sanctuary and see what I can do about training him. I've never turned anyone myself, but my maker was a good role model. Hopefully I can emulate him."

"What became of your maker? Did he resist you leaving him?"

"Keres happened," Dorchester said bitterly. "My maker enjoyed seeing the world but he respected my medical ambitions and let me remain here while he went off. One year, he simply didn't come back. I investigated the last place where I knew he'd been, and found a local vampire, in Keres' control. He told me she'd torn my maker apart and absorbed his blood spirit because he had a talent over air that she didn't."

"How awful."

"Apparently she has an idea or fetish about expanding the circle of her powers."

"Circle?" The word triggered Taviano's memories from Malik's transformation. The demon inside him felt alert as well. This was important, somehow.

"I think the term her slave used was 'squaring the circle'."

THIRTEEN

Paul

PAUL CROUCHED DOWN next to Nonna, who had wrapped herself in one of the blankets over his jacket and her housecoat. "Don't worry, Taviano will get to us soon," he said with great confidence.

"What makes you think this…this *gay vampire* will risk his life for you?" Gianni asked in a scathing voice.

"He loves me. Like you used to, only without conditions," Paul retorted.

"So uncool, Uncle Gianni," Luca put in. "Gay, straight, everything in between. It's all beautiful, man. Love in any form is beautiful."

"Are you stoned right now?" Gianni demanded. "We're being held prisoner, we're probably all going to be dead soon, and you're talking about *love*?"

"I had just taken a really good gummy when that Jet Li-wannabe grabbed me."

"You got any more gummies?" Sofia asked. "I think I'd rather not be thinking the things I'm thinking right now."

"Sorry, cuz, I put the tin away just before."

"Paulie, are you sure it's love?" Nonna sounded troubled.

"Of course it is!" Paul protested. "You've met Taviano. There isn't an insincere bone in his hot body."

"I didn't know he was Taviano Adelfio," Nonna said, the last name sounding like a curse in her mouth. "The pain he caused my grandfather. I don't know, Paulie. These creatures seem awfully fixated on our family. Now it turns out Taviano was not only with my grandfather but also my grandson. Couldn't it be that Taviano is with you for the same reason these other vampires took us?"

"That... Well, I don't even know what to say about that," Paul huffed and turned away to look up at the bank of windows. "It's ridiculous," he added for good measure.

He wished his voice hadn't cracked at the end there. Because suddenly he was remembering last Christmas Eve, when he'd been bleeding out on that rooftop. He'd seen Taviano going down on his knees as three vampires tried to kill him, and then he'd *felt* it when the bloodbeast inside had taken over. The ichor in Paul's body had responded like an orchestra tuning up to the *1812 Overture*. The thing zipping around the rooftop in Taviano's body, power almost tangible in the air as it dispatched two of the attackers, had been terrifying.

And then it had turned and looked at him. There was a moment as Paul struggled to his feet, neck and chest wet with his own blood, when he'd been sure the thing was going to attack him next. Their eyes had met, and whoever or whatever was behind those eyes... Well, it hadn't been Taviano.

And then, suddenly, it *was* again. The beast had withdrawn or retreated or whatever it did, and Taviano was back, rushing across the rooftop to hold Paul tight and sob with relief that he was alive.

Taviano loved him, Paul had zero doubts about that. But the bloodbeast? Who really knew how and why it had somehow brought Taviano thousands of miles to Boston to connect with the descendant of his onetime boyfriend Calogero. Okay, not boyfriend, but hookup at least.

"Find me, Taviano," he whispered to the wall, suddenly cold.

Sofia wrapped her arms around him, then rested her head on his shoulder. "Aunt Conchetta is a smart cookie, but I think she's wrong about this. I saw you guys together. To Taviano, you're the most precious thing on Earth."

"Thanks," Paul said, blinking back tears. "You're a smart cookie, too."

Luca wandered up to them. "Can I get some of that hugging action? My gummy is wearing off, I think, and I'm starting to get what a shitshow this might be."

"Sure," Paul grinned and opened his arms, wrapping one around his taller and younger cousin. Sofia drew him in from the other side, and the three huddled together in the cold, dank room. Gianni sniffed ostentatiously, muttered something, and paced the wall on the opposite side of the room.

Nonna got up and came over, trailing the blanket. She tossed it around the trio, fussing and tucking.

"Now you'll get cold, Nonna," Paul protested.

"I'll be fine. Boston winters have made me a tough old bird." She reached up to tousle Paul's hair.

Something electric shot from her fingers at the first touch, down through Paul's head and body and out to his fingertips. He was on fire for a moment, and then ice water ran in his veins. A current ran up and down his body, but on the inside. In the moment it took him to process what he was feeling, Sofia gasped, and Nonna all but vibrated in agitation.

"What the fuck?" Luca choked out. "What's happening?"

"Language," Nonna said, but her teeth were chattering.

"It's the ichor!" Paul shouted. He realized the way they were standing, four people somehow marked by these vampires for a mysterious shared quality, all touching. "It's that quintessence shit. Something's happening. Dad, get your ass over here."

Gianni choked out a cry and when Paul looked, his father had his back pressed to the opposite wall. "You're all... What's wrong with you? Ma, get away from them!"

His face was strangely visible in the dark cell, ghostly in a reflected blue glow. Paul suddenly realized a light was growing in the cell, and coming from their cluster of bodies. He looked at his own hand, at Nonna's face. Her ancient skin seemed like a translucent mineral now, a light from inside showing capillaries and bones yet rendering her beautiful. Sofia and Luca also shone with inner light.

Sofia jerked away in shock, breaking the connection. Immediately the light began to fade.

Paul grabbed for her hand and yelled, "Dad, we need you! Right now!"

"Son, vieni qui," Nonna said more calmly. One hand still on Paul, she extended the other and gestured. Reluctantly, Gianni crossed the room to take the hand.

When all five were connected, the glow seemed even brighter. A feeling grew in Paul's belly, like excitement and nausea and happiness and joy so big he couldn't contain it, so terrible that it made him afraid. It was like falling in love and losing the person in the same instant, great and huge and beyond anything he knew how to handle. Sofia's wide eyes, Luca's slack jaw—he could tell he wasn't the only one feeling it. Nonna's eyes were closed and her lips were tight. Gianni moaned.

A throb deep in Paul's body caught his attention. He closed his eyes; behind the lids, it was as if he could see the ichor remaining in him. It formed a web of blue light that also sang through his veins and arteries, pulsing, stretched taut and...waiting?

Without hands or any other means he could name, Paul reached toward the thickest strand of the light in his body, which somehow connected his head and his heart. The light had substance. Crystal, silk, mercury—he couldn't even articulate what it reminded him of. It was unique and familiar, alien but comforting. It was *not* him but it *waited* for him to do...something.

This was ichor, he remembered, as if emerging from a dream. This was the tangible evidence of Taviano's love for him, the result of their *making* love.

Paul pulled on the column of blue light with his own love, striking a pure note as if he had plucked on a harp string. Instead of fading away, though, the note swelled, the column of light thickened, and Paul felt Nonna's hand tighten on him.

"Hold on!" he said, afraid she would pull back. He seemed to be shouting to his family, because even though part of his mind knew the cell was silent, all he could hear was the pure note of music. Somehow it even sounded blue, growing and reaching parts of his soul that didn't need ears.

Luca's voice, sounding thick and full of tears, cut through the sweet roar. "It's so beautiful I don't know if I can stand it."

"Almost there." It was Sofia, and while Paul didn't know what she meant, he was sure she was right.

Gianni tried to pull free, to break the circuit. "No, son," Nonna said to him, but gently. "Don't be afraid. Just...a moment more..."

And the sound broke, a wave of blue light and song that washed outward from them and through the walls of the cell in every direction, spreading into the night.

Released from its power, the five people let go of each other, blinking away an afterimage that had nothing to do with their again-dark cell, shaking their heads to clear the ringing in their ears from the soundless crescendo they had just birthed.

Only then did Paul wonder, who else would be able to hear that music?

FOURTEEN

Taviano

S QUARING THE CIRCLE. The words rang in Taviano's head and, even deeper, inside the bloodbeast that shared his body. What could it mean?

"Doctor, does the word quintessence mean anything to you?"

"Hm. It's used to mean something's essential element, or maybe the ultimate expression of a quality. And my Organic Chemistry professor mentioned it in connection with alchemy, from which modern chemistry derives. But I don't recall any details. Why do you ask?"

"When Malik was made three months ago, he only had a short time with his maker before she was destroyed by Cambridge. But she said to him that the 'quintessence is known', and the 'circle must grow before it can be squared'."

Rani frowned. "I have no idea what that means, though it sounds as if Malik's maker was perhaps after the same thing as Keres."

Taviano's demon was so agitated that he worried for a moment it would try to wrest control of his body. Silently, he willed it, *Please don't fight me. I understand, this is perhaps at the heart of why Paul was taken.*

The demon relented in its struggle, curling up inside Taviano, but like a large lion feigning rest. It was willing to remain a spectator for now, but ready to strike out at the slightest provocation.

To Dorchester, he said, "My bloodbeast drew me to Paul. Nearly two centuries ago, I was close with one of his ancestors, so I almost couldn't believe it when Paul turned out to be of Calogero's line. I thought that my bloodbeast just didn't want me to be lonely anymore, but what if it was more than that? What if Paul is this 'quintessence' and tied to the queen's plans?"

A slight breeze stirred the air then as Malik returned. His grin showed he had been successful.

"Good job," Dorchester said, resting a hand on his shoulder.

"Are we going after Paul now?" the boy asked. Dorchester had just begun to shake her head no, when Malik pointed and yelled, "Wait, what the fuck is *that*?"

Taviano and Dorchester turned as one. Both gaped at a glowing wave of blue rushing straight at them. It was a mile away and already the thick band was clearly taller than a person.

It was half a mile away before Taviano realized it wasn't water or even pure light, but something that shimmered as it came at them.

It was ten feet away and had to be three stories tall. Swirling on itself like a bolt of silk or water pouring over a cliff and plunging into a gorge...

And then it collided with the trio of vampires.

Pure music swept through every fibre of Taviano's being. No, not even music. A single note of piercing sweetness that still somehow told of cerulean skies, midnight-dark waters deep in a cavern, a sapphire-studded wall shimmering in torchlight.

A man in a green robe stood behind a table on which was spread an assortment of tools—a glass rod, vials, a hammer and knife.

The man spoke to someone Taviano couldn't see. "This is our real innovation. The material must be broken and shattered into its component parts. Each element, free of the corrupting effect of the alloy, will be distilled to its purest and most perfect form. Then we will square the circle as we apply the quintessence. And from the dross—the lead, if you will—we will possess the pure gold…"

The man's voice faded behind a roar of fury. Rage swept through Taviano, but it was an echo of the blue note. Its song now was of hope betrayed, of the sorrow of glimpsed freedom that was ripped away, of a burning anger and hunger for revenge. The rage swelled until it abruptly became the pain of tearing and ripping, the loss of a name, an important and powerful name gone, the raw exposure and fear of powerlessness. So empty and lost.

What am I for? How do I avenge myself?

A male in rich robes, clutching his heart as he fell. A woman sprawled across a bed, blood soaking the sheets as a baby was lifted from her dead body. A youth in a dark alley, sinking to his knees as the knife in his gut finished its job. A female in servant garb, face purple above the hands that had tightened inexorably around her neck.

And then, for the briefest moment, a different baby. A different room. The first cry of angry little lungs, and I feel the pattern, see the possible shape of things to come.

As it joined to the baby, and before it lost itself in the dream of a newborn, the last echo of the blue note sang of hope.

Taviano was on his hands and knees. Dimly, he realized Dorchester and Malik were down as well. No more than a second seemed to have passed. He looked quickly over his shoulder, just in time to see the wave of blue vanish into the distance as it continued to expand. The afterimage in his eyes was of a ring of glowing energy that had spread in all directions outward, from some point north and west of where they were. A few humans walking through the park seemed utterly unaware of what had just passed by.

"Did you see…?" Malik began.

"A man. The dead. A baby." Dorchester spoke slowly, as if in a trance. "Listen," she said in a different voice. "Listen to your blood spirit."

Only then did Taviano realize his bloodbeast was utterly silent, as it hadn't been since the moment Bronislav put it into his body. He turned his awareness inward.

Demon? he probed. *Do you know what that was?*

No answer came, either in feelings or in words.

He let himself sink deeper, closing his physical eyes but opening his heart and mind to seek the thing that kept those organs functioning. Finally, he sensed a tremor. Concentrating hard, he followed it deeper down. Even in his imagination, the core of him was dark and echoing, lit faintly by a pale smudge of yellow and green that hung in the air.

The essence that had driven him for more than one hundred seventy years, the mighty creature that had torn apart its enemies and claimed the North End, huddled and shivered. It had drawn so completely in on itself that Taviano could almost see its shape, a faint shimmer in the darkness.

Why he did it, Taviano was ever after uncertain. The fear and hopelessness of the vision resonated still in his bloodbeast, reducing it to this lost thing. He called it his demon, but in truth it had been his companion for years, decades, nearly one and three-quarter centuries. It wasn't a demon; it was his blood spirit. And it was afraid.

He spread his mental arms in an invitation and sent a welcome to the shimmer. "We are one. You gave me back my hope when you brought me to Paul. Let me give you hope."

The smudge drifted closer, slowly at first, then brushing against Taviano's thoughts. No words came, but a tentative question. He felt the certainty of his answer even as he framed it in his head.

Yes, we are together. You are not lost. We are home.

The shimmer grew brighter as Taviano repeated his thoughts, as reassuring as he could be. The blood spirit relaxed and spread, losing its color and definition as it drifted larger. Soon it was the same size as him, then it dwarfed him. Yet Taviano felt cocooned as the thing grew, even as he reassured it.

He opened his eyes again. Dorchester and Malik were still looking northwest, where the wave had come from. Malik had a hand over his heart, and his eyes shone.

He spotted Taviano watching him and beamed. "My passenger spoke to me. It told me I'm special and it chose me."

Dorchester nodded. "Mine spoke as well. Can you guess what word it shared with me?"

Taviano hadn't heard a word, but he knew exactly what she meant. He raised a hand and pointed to the origin of the wave of energy.

"Quintessence."

FIFTEEN

Paul

THE DOOR TO the cell slammed against the wall, thrown open so hard that something crunched. Paul instinctively stepped in front of Nonna.

"What did you do?" Bronislav bellowed. "The bloodbeast—it is terrified."

The one with Chinese features appeared next to him, fangs bared. "The baby. The king. What does it mean? My spirit is making me feel nonsense." He shoved his way past Bronislav. "I don't care how important you are. You can be just as useful with fewer arms and legs."

Luca shook his head. "Dude, I don't know what you're talking about."

"We didn't see anything about kings or babies," Sofia said from next to him. Paul realized they'd joined him to make a line in front of Nonna and Gianni. It might be ageist or sexist, but they would do what they could and apologize later.

From above came that low voice Paul had already learned to hate. "Back away, Cambridge," the female vampire hissed. "All that has happened is all that we need to happen."

"Speak plainly, Keres," Bronislav demanded. "We gathered these humans as you wanted but you have explained nothing.

What did they do, and why is my bloodbeast reacting?"

The female—Keres, Paul figured—did that creepy-ass thing again where she slithered down the wall to the floor, then somehow reared herself to standing without appearing to move a muscle. Gianni made a noise of disgust, and Keres shot a malevolent glance his way.

"Don't annoy the vampire, Dad," Paul said out of the side of his mouth. "It won't end well for you."

Keres grinned hugely, letting her fangs catch what light came into the cell. "Listen to your child, human. We can find more of your line if we get annoyed and one of you must be…replaced."

Returning her attention to Bronislav, she said impatiently, "Your soul guest is unharmed. It is merely subdued by revelation."

"Revelation of what?" the vampire she called Cambridge asked, and Paul finally recognized him as one of the attackers from Christmas. "I didn't understand anything I just saw, and my spirit is radiating gibberish."

"Tell me," Keres demanded. "Put into words what your spirit is telling you."

Cambridge shook his head as if to clear it. "It makes no sense. Betrayal, babies, it must have tools if it is ever to regain the sky…"

"A cavern and a lake," Bronislav added. "So deep that the light of the sun has never reached it."

"Ah, your soul guest has stirred and wants more than blood," Keres said. "And yet you do not see. Did you not recognize any of the dead bodies in the vision?"

Cambridge crooked his head to look at her. Narrowed his eyes. "The woman in servant garb. I think you'd been strangled."

Bronislav began to scoff, but stopped when Keres hissed a laugh.

"Yes, that was me. And still you don't understand." She drift-ed closer to the two vampires, who cringed minutely. Although they towered above her, there was no doubt they feared the tiny woman.

"What you witnessed was the birth of our race, the race of vampires. I was a slave in a household in Florence, taken from my home in Greece and sold as a child. The chief steward tried to force himself on me, so I drove a little dagger into his thigh. He responded by strangling me to death. I can still recall the sensation of dying, the darkness, the panic. My fury, and need for revenge. And just as the last spark of my life was fading, some-thing joined me. I felt it settle over me like a shroud, my kalesménos psychí. My soul guest. My rage became strength, and I tore that steward to pieces. My fangs, the need for blood…that all came later. In that first moment, I was an unformed host for vengeance, and I began by murdering every member of the family that enslaved me, from the oldest grandfather to the youngest babe."

She spread her arms, palms to the ceiling as she looked sky-ward. Paul was reminded of statues of the Virgin Mary.

"I was the first chosen, as you saw," Keres said dreamily. "And thus I am your queen."

"I saw three others 'chosen' as well," Cambridge said nastily. "Don't they have the same claim? For that matter, you weren't even the first one—"

He gasped, his words choking off. It took Paul a moment to see that Keres had sped at Cambridge and buried her nails in his chest. Cambridge tried to struggle back, but in less than a second she had broken through his ribcage to rip out his heart. Cam-bridge crumpled to the floor, but the heart—still imbued with ichor—continued to beat in Keres' outstretched hand. She contemplated it for a moment, then brought it to her mouth. In some fashion Paul couldn't understand, she unhinged her jaw and shoved the organ in whole.

Behind him, Gianni vomited.

Keres fixed her gaze on Bronislav. "And do you have any question about my right to rule?"

Bronislav stood rigid for a moment, then slowly, looking reluctant, he folded himself into a bow. "My queen," he said in a tight voice.

Keres turned then to face Paul and his family. Nonna clutched the back of his shirt as if to restrain him, but Paul couldn't move even if he wanted to. What she had done to the vampire... If Taviano came to the rescue, the same thing would happen to him. Fervently, Paul prayed that Taviano would stay far, far away, no matter what happened.

But he had his family to think of as well. If he pissed Keres off, well, they'd already said other members of the family could be dragged in to replace him. Next time it might be cousin Tony's new baby.

Sofia must have been thinking along the same lines. She cleared her throat, and when she spoke, it sounded respectful. "Look, uh, your majesty. We don't understand anything that's going on. We didn't see a vision. Don't you think we could be more useful if you explained it to us?"

"The culmination is at hand. More than seven hundred fifty years have passed since I was reborn. From the beginning... I *knew*. The entity that chose me has spread its kingdom across this Earth. Its children are legion, and we war with each other ceaselessly. Once I complete its purpose, though, I will ascend. I will be master of all vampires, and I will unite them. Together we will impose our will on the daylight world, and tear down the false gods it worships."

"You mean like the Kardashians? Ow!" Luca exclaimed as

Paul elbowed him in the ribs.

But Keres was not distracted. Her eyes shone with a red light. "I have found the quintessence, the fifth element that the entity hid away in a living babe at the same moment it restored my dead body. I was imbued by it with the mastery of Water. Then I found and consumed those few of us given mastery of Fire and Air. All that remains to be found is a vampire with mastery of Earth, the rarest gift of all. With the four alchemical elements at my command, and the quintessence at my mercy, I will square the circle. I will solve the riddle put down by the alchemists."

She pulled forth from her tracksuit top a necklace on a golden chain. Hanging from it was a charm. Paul squinted in the poor light and leaned forward. It seemed to be made of silver and formed a pattern, a circle surrounded by a square, itself surround-ed by a triangle and finally that contained in a larger circle:

Distracted by the shiny figure, it took a moment for Keres' ravings to penetrate Paul's mind. Mastery of Earth. Malik. *Holy shit.*

He tried very hard to relax his shoulders before Keres could catch on. If she suspected he knew something valuable, he had no doubt she'd be able to force him to reveal it, most likely by torturing one of his cousins even if she had to go kidnap another family member afterward.

Nonna scoffed behind him. "É il tuo grande piano? Your big plan is to take the world back to some point in the mythical past?"

"What are you doing, Ma? Don't aggravate the crazy lady," Gianni whispered frantically.

Nonna ignored him and pushed her way past Paul. "Myth. That's all this is, right? Even if you are that old, you're just guessing."

"Woman, I will rip your tongue from your head if you utter one more word," Keres hissed.

"Do it," Nonna dared. "I'm the oldest one in the family since my sister Carla died, may she rest in peace. Each generation gets weaker, right? So if you kill me, who's to say you'll ever be able to find enough of us to do your quintessence bullshit."

"Nonna!" Paul gasped, more shocked at the rare swearword than that she was antagonizing a monster.

"She's right," came a deep voice. Keres whirled on Bronislav. He held up his palms. "Neither I nor Cambridge sensed the quintessence in the other family members we located. She and the boy"—he gestured at Nonna and Paul—"have the strongest traces of it. These others collectively have no more than the boy alone."

Keres quivered, apparently torn between punishing the woman who dared speak back to her, and accepting Bronislav's words.

In her hesitation, Bronislav continued. "We have them, we can keep them here, until you locate one with the remaining elemental control."

"Not here," Keres snapped. "The North End might find them, or even gather allies. We must take them out of this forsaken country."

"Back to Florence then," Bronislav said with a bow. "To your demesne."

"I will contact my familiars at once to make the preparations. No doubt it will be another day before we can remove them."

"Shall I provide food and water, or would you rather let them think how best to address you in the future?"

Nonna spoke up. "I'm an old woman with diabetes and other mortal weaknesses. If I don't get some decent food and water soon, I might die."

Keres gave a grunt of disgust, and waved a hand imperiously. "Give them something. It will be easier to deal with them tomorrow." With that, she took Cambridge's corpse by the foot, moved to the wall and rose back into the shadows.

Paul watched her climb, as creepily fascinated as the first time. "Suppose she's going to snack on the rest of that guy?" he muttered.

When he turned back, though, he froze. Bronislav was staring straight at him, a slight and sinister smile stretching his face. He pointed a finger at Paul and shook his head. Then he mouthed the words, "You know something."

Bronislav left, clanging the heavy door shut behind him. But Paul had no doubt he'd be back soon, and then what would he do?

SIXTEEN

Taviano

TAVIANO SPED ACROSS the miles separating him from the source of that beacon. From rooftop to rooftop he leapt, past suburban homes that gave way to older styles and then to buildings. For the beacon had called him, Dorchester and Malik to come, and they answered.

The other two vampires did their best to keep up, but Taviano was possessed with certainty that drove him ever faster. Whatever the quintessence was, it had sent out that summons. And somehow, he was sure, where the quintessence was, he would find his Paul.

The Lord help Bronislav and whoever had aided him.

The bloodbeast—no, the blood *spirit*—shared his certainty. Behind him, Malik gave a small cry as he apparently missed his jump. Taviano called a wind that scooped up the boy and got him to the next surface. The magic was effortless, with none of the struggle he was used to when his blood spirit fought for control. For once, they were united in their goals and their need.

Emboldened, he let the magic flow more wildly. Unlike the last time he'd given the spirit free reign, his own consciousness remained in control. The wind in his face became a wind at his back, pushing him and the other two vampires faster and faster until it lifted them off their feet entirely. Dorchester called out this time in alarm, but Malik gave a whoop. It reminded Taviano of Paul's excitement on Christmas Eve, when they had run so fast it had felt to Paul like they were flying.

We are flying now, my love. To your side.

The blood spirit thrummed its agreement as they neared the Charles River. City lights reflected in the water looked like a carnival show. Even at the late hour, a few boats plied their way along the water. On the other side rose the town of Cambridge. In order to avoid conflict with the vampire who claimed it, Taviano had never been there before that night. But if Cambridge was in league with Bronislav and had helped him take Paul, then they were already at war.

The wind he commanded spread ripples along the river as the trio of vampires crossed. Distantly, he heard curses from boat captains but not real alarm, so they sped on.

"There," Dorchester called out as they passed onto land once more. He glanced her way and saw she was pointing to an area that was conspicuously dark among the otherwise well-lit streets. "My spirit feels the call there."

Taviano's agreed, and the wind carried them over the town and toward the darkened area. As they neared it, Taviano could make out beautiful parklands, dotted with obelisks and monuments of stone and marble. It was a cemetery, he realized. He let the wind slow and bring them to alight in a copse of trees.

"Why'd we stop?" Malik asked. "The call came from ahead." Taviano followed Malik's pointing finger to a stone tower that rose from the cemetery grounds.

"I know," he said. "We need to assess the situation as best we can before we engage."

"If whoever is in there didn't already feel your small hurricane," Dorchester grumbled. "All right, I have this trick. I don't really know how it works—something about muffling the presence of one of us. I suspect Keres knows it as well." She stretched out her hands and immediately a flurry of diamonds rose from the grass to sparkle around her in the scarce light of the cemetery.

No, not diamonds. It's dew!

As Dorchester had said, Taviano discovered he couldn't *feel* her at all. He could see her with his eyes, but the usual vibration of another vampire simply wasn't there. The sudden absence felt very much like when Bronislav had disappeared with Paul from Taviano's senses. Without another word, Dorchester slipped forward in the darkness, toward the tower.

"Will she be okay?" Malik asked in a whisper.

"I hope so."

It was disconcerting not to be able to track Dorchester's movements. The seconds passed agonizingly, turning into long minutes. Malik shifted next to him once or twice, and Taviano bit back the urge to command him to stillness. The boy was as nervous as he was, and unprepared for what could turn into a battle between powerful supernatural creatures.

"Malik, I think you should leave and hide," Taviano said. "You know how to get into my lair. I'd like you to go there and wait. If we don't return, well…"

"No fuckin' way," Malik growled back. "I said I'd help you get Paul. And anyway, my spirit is invested in this. Whatever sent the summons…that isn't something it can ignore."

"Then hang back—"

He was interrupted by Dorchester as she stepped out of the darkness. He hadn't heard or felt her coming.

"Under the Washington tower," she said, gesturing toward the stone monument. "There's a small window and through it I could see the blond boy I believe is your familiar, and four other mortals."

Paul, I'm coming, he vowed. "Five humans! All being kept together?"

"There's more," Dorchester said. "The call came from that room. I sensed...something. A *quality* in the room centered on the mortals. I can't explain it, but the five of them, all gathered together? It can't be a coincidence."

"What are you saying?"

"It's a guess, but my blood spirit seems to think that, collectively, they are the quintessence."

"That kind of makes sense," Malik said. "Quint is five, right?"

Well, it made no sense to Taviano. In the months he'd been with Paul, he'd had no inkling that there was something supernatural about him.

Or had he missed the signs?

Blood spirit, exactly why did you choose Paul, of all people, for me?

No answer rose in his mind, but was that a sense of...satisfaction?

Demon, answer me! Is Paul tied to you in some way?

The blood spirit didn't answer in words, but a flood of images filled Taviano's mind. Paul's immediate acceptance of him. His fearlessness at having invited a vampire into his home. His certainty that Taviano was not damned but something more. And the shocking discovery that Paul was a descendant of long-dead Calogero...

"Do you have any idea who the other mortals are?" Taviano asked, frowning.

"The one I think is Paul called an elderly woman, 'Nonna'."

Taviano's hands flew to his mouth. "Nonna? They took Paul's *grandmother*, too?"

"That's fucked up," Malik muttered.

"It's his bloodline," Taviano gasped, suddenly seeing it. "Nearly two hundred years ago, I knew Paul's ancestor. My blood spirit caused me to come to Boston and put us in Paul's path. I thought it was a kindness to me, but it had its own agenda. Nearly all of Paul's family lives in the North End, including his grandmother. The other three—I wager they are his relatives, too."

"What's so special about his bloodline?" Malik asked.

Yes, demon. Tell me now! Taviano thought, enraged. *What is so special about Paul's family?*

An image appeared in his mind, a fragment of the vision they'd all shared when the blue beacon passed through them. A newborn baby. A shred of something, coalescing and joining with the infant...

"Paul is descended from the baby we saw," Taviano said. "The one claimed however many hundreds of years ago. Paul's grandmother, too, and I suppose other members of his family."

Pain seared his soul. Did Paul's mystical, impossible connection to the blood spirits mean *that* was what drew him? Did he love Taviano of his own will, or was it something the blood spirits caused?

Did *he* love Paul, or did the demon force them together? Tears blinded his eyes suddenly, and his heart ached.

Did you cause this? Answer me, God damn you, or I will find a way to walk into the sunrise and end your existence.

NO

For only the second time in their decades together, Taviano heard his blood spirit's words.

I CHOSE YOU BECAUSE OF YOUR LOVE FOR A SOUL BEARER. I DREW YOU TO ANOTHER SOUL BEARER BECAUSE THE TIME APPROACHES AND BECAUSE YOU NEEDED HIM. BUT THE REST—I DID NOT CAUSE IT TO

HAPPEN

"I wish I could believe you," Taviano whispered.

"What's that?" Dorchester asked.

Taviano just shook his head. Throat thick with his choked-back doubts and fears, he managed to ask, "Did you identify other vampires?"

"I felt only one other but... I don't know." Dorchester hesitated. "The thing I do with water, muffling my presence. There was a hint of the same magic coming from inside the monument. I can't be sure, but I think there's at least one other vampire inside. If so, it's likely the queen."

Taviano looked eastward. Luckily, given the time of year, dawn was still about an hour away. He was wracked by doubt, though. What approach would keep Paul the safest? They could attack in force, and hope the three of them were more powerful than the two or three inside. They could wait another day, try to recruit help from other vampires. He could slip in alone, and ask Dorchester and Malik to stand by on reserve.

"How close to the outer wall would you say the humans were?" Malik asked Dorchester.

"Very close, but below ground level."

"Do you think you could use your trick to muffle both of us at the same time?"

Dorchester cocked her head, considering. "Yes, I believe so. Let's find out." Stepping close to Malik, she raised her hand and spread her fingers. Again, droplets of night-forming dew rose like a spray of glitter in reverse. In seconds, both she and Malik were encased.

"Well?" she asked Taviano.

He nodded his head. "It works. I see you but I can't *feel* either of you."

"Here's my idea," Malik said. "Dorchester gets the two of us close, I use my trick to open a hole in the earth around the tower and then into the basement. Then we hustle the humans the fuck out of there, as fast as we can."

"You might as well call me Rani, since we're apparently going into battle together," she said. "It's risky. But yes, they shouldn't feel us coming. Once you start moving earth, though, they're likely to sense that one way or another."

Malik pointed at Taviano. "That's where you come in, big guy."

"I see. I go knock on the front door while you sneak in the back."

"Right on."

Taviano forced out a shaky breath. Given what Dorchester—well, Rani—had told them about Keres, and the fact she might have at least two vampire allies... There was little chance of them surviving this attack. He wanted very much to keep Rani and Malik out of the fight, but they had both apparently felt summoned and wouldn't listen to him. Besides, what meager chance he had to get Paul to safety could only improve with their help.

If this was his last night, so be it. As long as Paul survived, then he would go to his damnation still glad of having accomplished one, important task.

"All right. I see no better plan. I'll go in as flashily as I can." He paused. "One thing, please. Paul is the most important thing in my world, and his grandmother is the most important thing in his. Whatever is in motion for our kind turns on them as well. I beg you, if you can get them away, do so even if it means abandoning me."

Taviano's blood spirit surged inside him, on alert. Alarm flickered along their connection.

"I will not sacrifice myself easily or willingly," Taviano continued, both for his compatriots and his spirit. "But I am not the priority."

Rani nodded. "Agreed."

"Go be a badass," Malik said. "We've got this."

Despite himself, Taviano smiled. Malik's confidence reminded him of Paul's. He was sure the two would be good friends, if everyone lived through the night.

Closing his eyes, he sank into communion with his blood spirit.

We are together now, yes? Our goals are aligned. When I cede control, no one but the vampires who took Paul or try to keep him from us will be harmed.

It wasn't a question, but he sensed the spirit respond with calm assurance.

Then, as Malik says, let's be a badass.

It began as warmth, such an unusual sensation for a vampire. The heat kindled and grew in his chest as the spirit flexed the fire gift Taviano had absorbed when he—*when the blood spirit*—had killed the prior master of the North End. Even as his limbs grew hotter, he heard the leaves around them rustle. A breeze brushed his fevered cheek, and quickly grew into a wind, then a gale. The trees in the cemetery copse creaked and bent as the power of Taviano's storm surged, dry leaves rustling as they swirled around and around. The wind whistled. As the fire in his hands grew into a blaze, the rage in his heart swelled to a fever pitch.

He was dimly aware of Rani and Malik stepping back, out of the range of his storm. *Good. Spirit, let us draw the eyes of those who wronged us and ours. Let them feel our wrath.*

The leaves caught in his winds burst into flame from the rising heat, and Taviano drifted up in the center of his cyclone.

They took Paul from us! he thought, no longer sure if the words were his or the blood spirit's. *THEY WILL PAY*

More debris was sucked in and immediately blazed up, until he found himself in the center of a true firestorm.

SOUL SHRIVEN! PRETENDER! FALSE!

He didn't know if his body actually howled the words out loud, but he was certain that whatever was inside the stone monument had heard. Then, like a bullet from a gun, he hurled himself at the tower. The door exploded inward, filling the room beyond with shattered glass and splintered wood.

And there in the middle of the room, waiting for him, stood Bronislav and a tiny woman, power radiating from her.

The vampire queen.

SEVENTEEN

Paul

PAUL'S HEAD SHOT up at the explosion of noise somewhere above their cell. The voice roaring was one he'd heard before, when Taviano's demon had taken over last Christmas and obliterated two vampires.

"Taviano found us!" he chortled, eyes on the ceiling. "And holy shit, those fuckers are in trouble now."

Nonna pressed close to him. "Is it just him? Can he really fight those other two monsters?"

"He's got a lot of mojo when he lets his demon-thingy come out to play," Paul said confidently. He winced involuntarily as something heavy crashed above them, and fought the urge to call out to Taviano, determined not to distract him.

"Should we do something to help?" Sofia asked.

"Like what?" Gianni said, getting up from the floor where he'd sagged after Bronislav left. "These things are evil. Unless you've got a cross or holy water…"

"Taviano isn't evil," Paul hissed, whirling on his father. "I've been inside St. Stephen's with him. He goes to Mass all the time."

"Let's hope he earned some favors from the angels then," Luca said. Above them, a deep male voice cried out in pain. "That wasn't our guy, was it?"

"No," Paul said firmly. "Bronislav. I'm sure of it." Another cry sounded, enraged. "*That* was Taviano."

Nonna tugged at his shirt, drawing his attention away from the ceiling and the sounds of the fight above. "Paulie, something's happening outside the window."

He turned to look, then pulled Nonna back and away from the outside wall as bits of concrete fell away from the surface. A spiderweb crack widened and became a hole, and then the wall seemed to crumble in on itself. Chunks of it disappeared, pulled away from the building they were in. In moments, an opening four feet tall had formed. Beyond the concrete, they could see earth had been scooped out as if by a backhoe. Stars glinted in the night sky.

"Paul? Are you all okay?" a voice whispered. A head blocked the sky and appeared in the opening. "It's Malik. We've got to go. Right now."

Gianni scrambled for the opening immediately, hands slipping in the dirt as he started to work his way through.

"Nice," Paul scoffed. "Don't let your elderly mother go first or anything."

"Who are you calling elderly?" Nonna said, lightly slapping the side of his head. She turned and looked at the door to their cell. "Uh oh."

The sounds of battle had changed. No longer coming from above, they grew closer and closer. Another shriek, female this time, indicated Keres was in the battle. Even Gianni paused in his scurrying out.

The cell door exploded. The furious mass of flame and wind that burst into the cell was almost incomprehensible. Flickers—a hand shaped into a claw, a white face, fangs—revealed themselves. It took Paul a moment to realize he was seeing three vampires, unfettered and unrestrained, trying to tear one another apart.

A huge male sagged to the floor, so scratched that Paul barely realized it was Bronislav before he returned to the fight. The battle raged on, though flame and smoke made it impossible to judge if Taviano was all right. A shout of *PRETENDER* made Paul cover his ears as Keres flew backwards out of the melee to smash against the wall.

Her clothing was in shreds, her face streaked with ichor, but her fangs were bared in a terrible rage. She was about to launch herself back into the fray when she seemed to catch sight of the mortals.

And the opening in the wall.

And the small vampire above, holding back the ground.

"Earth gift!" she screeched and rushed toward the opening instead of the fight.

"Taviano!" Paul shouted at the same time. "Stop her!"

The fight paused just long enough for Paul to spy Taviano and Bronislav locked in combat, both covered in gashes and streaks of ichor. Flame danced along their bodies, not consuming their clothes. Taviano made a fist and a pulling motion; instantly a wind rushed inward, carrying Malik's chunks of displaced tower and rock right into Keres' face. The blast sent her reeling back into the room.

Taviano was on her in an instant, his hands around her throat. But tiny though she was, Keres pushed him away. He flew up to the ceiling, crashing into it, then falling facedown on the floor.

"Move," a new, female voice hissed. Suddenly another vampire entered the room through Malik's opening, her teeth bared and hands extended. Gianni scrambled out of her way.

Keres grimaced and froze in place as the new vampire made a drawing gesture with her hands. Sweat glistened on Keres' skin, and then began to pull away, forming globules of water in the air.

Malik slid into the room as well. "She's on our side," he said to Paul as he gestured at the newcomer.

"I got that. Help her!"

"Oh, uh. Yeah." Malik extended his own hands, and the floor of the cell around Keres bubbled and heaved. "Rani! Make quicksand!"

The new vampire nodded and gave a sharp downward gesture. The moisture she'd sucked from Keres splashed into Malik's dust and the combined mass of water and earth began to swirl.

Keres stumbled to her knees and started to sink. Paul thought for a moment it was all over. But then she wrenched a leg up and out of the sucking morass. She made a hurling motion, and Rani collapsed with a cry. Keres pulled the other leg free.

Before she could come after Malik again, a whirlwind of flame surrounded her. Through the blaze, Paul could see Taviano had regained his feet and was combining his tricks with air and fire. Keres' clothes smoldered and burned, and her hair caught. Flames danced along her skin but Paul could see her skin was healing almost as fast as it was consumed. A wide smile displayed her ghastly fangs as she began to move through the whirlwind, advancing on Taviano.

Strain etched his face, but everything he threw at Keres was brushed aside. She leapt at him, hands curled into claws. Taviano bellowed in pain as she slashed across his chest. Somehow, he was able to catch an arm and fling her against the concrete wall so hard it cracked. She slumped, stunned, and Taviano threw more rubble at her with a blast of wind. Keres caught one of the large chunks and hurled it back at Taviano. It struck his leg and he screamed in pain, falling to the ground.

Paul clenched his fist in impotent rage. What could he do? There must be something. Taviano was in terrible trouble, and it was Paul's fault. Whatever was in him and his family—that was what Taviano might die for. Paul moaned.

Keres was crouched above Taviano now, her hands around his throat. "Your gifts are powerful, little vampire, but they are nothing compared to mine. For centuries, I have tested and reached and expanded the glories of my soul guest. I am the first, the greatest of our kind. You who would resist me, learn the price for such insolence. And when your physical body is no more and your own soul guest is absorbed into my vast and glorious core, perhaps you will still have some shred of yourself left to witness my reign."

Her hands burst into flame, still wrapped around Taviano's neck. Wind whistled around the cell as Taviano struggled to free himself. The pit of quicksand rippled in the tempest, the morass of earth and water churned to mud. Keres dragged Taviano to the muck and thrust his head down into it.

Gianni groaned, momentarily distracting Paul. He had fallen as he got out of the way and now cradled his arm. The glance at his father made Paul cry out. The blue glow they'd summoned earlier was again visible around Gianni. He looked at his hands, and at Nonna and his cousins. All of them were illuminated.

"Grab hold!" he shouted, reaching blindly for his family. Maybe they could make another beacon, cause a distraction. *Something* to help Taviano. Anything.

Nonna touched Gianni's shoulder. Sofia and Luca each took one of Paul's hands. Nonna reached back with her free hand and placed it against Paul's chest.

The light flared, building like it had before. But it was different, too. Paul felt warmth moving from his hands and up his arms, spreading outward from his heart. It filled his body, rising into his head. It felt like his hair was standing on end, crackling in a field of energy.

He turned at Keres' shout of triumph. "The circle is squared!"

In the moments it had taken for the five to connect again, she'd pulled Taviano out of the quicksand pit again. He was on his back beneath her, and her hand was around his throat, crushing it.

"No!" Paul screamed. The light flared brighter but it didn't do anything. It seemed to be waiting for something.

Keres threw Taviano aside and faced the humans gathered together. She spread her hands wide.

"I've done it. The four gifts gathered. The quintessence unleashed. Now, ancient forefather who created our race and chose me as queen. Fulfill the promise of seven hundred fifty years!"

EIGHTEEN

Taviano

TAVIANO FOUGHT THE darkness that dragged him down, but there was just so much of it. Was Paul safe? Taviano hurt so much, he just didn't know. Through eyes he could barely open, he saw a glow spread and fill the room. Was this what dying as a vampire felt like? Was he dead already, and this was the beginning of what awaited him?

He managed to open one eye enough to see Paul shining like a star, connected to his family by a blue sheen. Wonder filled his heart. The light surrounding his lover coruscated from the ground to the top of his head, at one moment like waves, at the next dancing flames. It was so beautiful, like the glory of a remembered dawn. Whatever essence Rani had sensed had been closed to Taviano before, but at that moment, he understood. The thing resided in all five mortals, yet as he watched, the glow drained from the other four humans and came to rest in Paul's body.

The power residing in that light was titanic. Taviano was almost content to die, knowing that Paul had a means to protect himself.

He closed his eyes.

NOT WHEN WE ARE SO CLOSE. HOLD FAST, WARRI-OR MONK

I-I'll try, spirit.

BEHOLD THE QUINTESSENCE. OPEN YOUR EYES AND SEE WHAT THERE IS TO SEE

Wearily, Taviano let the blood spirit bully him into holding on. He heard Keres ranting and forced his eyes open again, struggling to move, to use his gifts, as she stalked closer to Paul and the others.

"I have solved the alchemist's riddle," she hissed, frustration plain in her tone. Rani and Malik moved to block the humans, looking grim but determined. Keres gestured contemptuously and they each flew sideways to smash into opposite walls.

Paul's eyes darted over his own body, at the rippling light coming from him, clearly trying to understand how to use it. He shook his hands, waved them, made hurling motions. Nothing happened, but the glow remained strong.

Keres laughed. "Don't be foolish. The quintessence knows me. I am its queen. Now…"—she reached with both arms for Paul—"give me my reward!"

"Gladly," a deep, male voice said. Bronislav. Taviano had all but forgotten him in the battle with Keres.

The Russian vampire sped forward from the darkest corner of the cell, two sharp, curved blades in his hands. Before Keres could even turn, he swung downward. The blades whistled as they cleaved her arms from her shoulders.

Keres screamed in rage. She whirled to face her attacker, all of her presence smashing outwards. Bronislav quailed for a moment, but then drew back his left arm and, with a vicious snarl, sliced through the air. Keres' head somersaulted up and over in an arc, spraying ichor. More gushed from her neck. The head bounced on the floor and rolled to a stop, glaring at Paul.

The eyes, wide with shock and fury, blinked. The mouth moved.

Bronislav dropped his swords and crouched over the rest of Keres' crumpled body and severed arms. Hands clenched, he drew on the ichor spattered on the ground and pouring from her neck and shoulder stumps. It oozed together like rivulets of water, forming a puddle, then a pool. He stood again, hands outstretched over the scintillating sphere of liquid, drawing it up toward himself.

Taviano realized Bronislav was doing what his own blood spirit had done when it gathered the essences of two dead vampires last Christmas. Absorbing those vampires' ichor had increased his power incredibly, and given him memories that still plagued him.

Taviano's blood spirit reached out, trying to claim Keres' ichor for itself. But the demon was too depleted from the battle and from its reckless use of wind and fire to wrest the prize away from Bronislav.

"Ho una brutta sensazione al riguardo," Nonna muttered from where she stood behind Paul, nodding at Bronislav.

"I get a bad feeling, too," Sofia agreed.

"Not him," Paul cried out. "It should be Taviano!"

At his words, the dancing light around him suddenly flared. It burst brilliantly from Paul's hands toward Bronislav and exploded in his face, pushing him to slam into the cell door. The light took form, cupping to catch the glittering ichor from Keres' destroyed body and limbs, creating a basin of shimmering liquid that glowed from within. The cup of light drifted to Taviano's prone body where he lay on his back, unable to move. It tilted and poured itself over his head, then his chest, and then his arms and legs.

Colder than mountain snow at midnight, the ichor sank into his skin, healing his damaged body and mind. It mended torn flesh, straightened a leg that he realized only then had been broken. His blood spirit welcomed the ichor with a feeling of triumph and satisfaction that surged the length of Taviano's body and back again.

But Taviano cringed, terrified of what was coming next.

Almost immediately, images and feelings surged in his mind. From his experience at Christmas, he knew what was happening: Along with Keres' ichor, he and his spirit were absorbing her essential memories and strength. But she was so much more powerful than the vampires he had previously defeated. Keres' blood spirit attacked his own, furious, fighting for control. With the host dead, her spirit tried to take control of Taviano's body and mind.

Gritting his teeth, he marshaled every bit of strength he could manage. All his mental tricks when he battled his own blood spirit—visualizing a container to hold Keres, then a metal safe, then a sealed tomb. Each image shattered under Keres' onslaught.

Lord help him, Taviano wasn't sure he had enough will remaining to resist her. His eyes opened, and immediately found Paul's. "Help me!" he groaned.

"Taviano!" Paul tore himself away from his family and rushed across the cell, his blue aura gone now. Taviano sighed as he felt himself lifted in Paul's arms. "Are you okay?"

"I…I don't know if I can control her," Taviano said. "I feel I am drowning. She is so strong…"

He forced his eyes to remain open as he drew in Paul's presence. Paul was *safe*. He was there with Taviano, cradling him. The love and fear in Paul's eyes burned so brightly that Taviano found new reserves of strength. This was real, what existed between them. Whatever the blood spirits planned, whatever their history, Paul and Taviano loved each other of their own will.

That certainty gave his spirit a foothold. It warred with Keres but gained a small, perhaps temporary, advantage. Slowly, slowly, Taviano felt his spirit surround and encapsulate the vampire queen's essence.

Bronislav cursed in Russian as he pushed himself away from the door against which he'd been hurled. "Fine. This is not how I wanted events to go, but we have learned a very valuable lesson, have we not?" He showed his teeth in something between a grimace and a grin. To Paul, he said, "Do not forget that I saved you *and* your demon lover tonight when I killed Keres."

And then he sped away.

Taviano tensed, trying to find the strength to follow, but Paul put a hand on his chest to hold him down. "Don't. You need time and I think he's gone."

"Do you have any idea what this was all about?" Taviano asked wearily.

Paul just shook his head. Over his shoulder, Taviano saw two of Paul's cousins helping Rani to her feet. Her face and arms were bruised, but the color was fading from purple already. She was clearly wounded but healing rapidly.

Malik stood uncertainly in the middle of the cell, but seemed mostly unhurt. He looked around the room, at the damage caused by fire, wind, earth and water. "The alignment is not right," he said, then blinked. He shook his head. "Why did I say that?"

Taviano murmured, "I have no idea."

"Dawn is close," Rani said. "I need to drink and get indoors."

"Will a little of my blood help?" Luca asked Rani, shocking Taviano. So he knew they were vampires? Rani was shocked too, by the expression on her face. "Seriously. You helped save us. If you can drink some without killing me, I figure I owe you."

"That is very kind," she said. Then she cocked her head. "Curious. Before, the five of you shared some undefinable quality. Now, it is all in that one." She gestured at Paul. "The rest of you no longer bear the quintessence."

"Well, fuck me," Paul said softly.

"I would love to," Taviano answered with a smile, then passed out.

. . .

HE DRIFTED DOWN, exhausted, aware of Keres' blood spirit still battling his own, trying to make him yet another piece of fractured soul in a mosaic whose final shape Taviano couldn't see. Images began to pour into his dream, memories from a long, vicious and cruel life. So many victims drained. So many vampires murdered brutally, their essence absorbed.

And beneath that was a human lifetime. A young girl captured as a slave and dragged from Greece to Rome. Degradation, a sale to a vile mistress, a new home in Florence. The attention of a slave overseer rejected, hands around her neck. Blackness consuming her, then a spark of green brilliance that burned away her very blood and left her with the memory of something not herself crying out, *A FRAGMENT UNTIL THE CIRCLE MAY BE SQUARED.*

"Is he awake?" That voice was real, but it didn't sound like Paul.

"I don't think so. He's… I don't know. Healing maybe? Look, he's smiling!"

"Maybe it's from hearing your voice. What should we do? I can feel the sun is close to rising."

A third voice. "We don't have time to deal with all this damage. Best we leave the humans with a mystery and get to shelter. Paul, is it? As the North End's familiar, will you give us sanctuary in your master's lair?"

"Uh, what? Oh, yes, sure. Nonna, Dad, you guys. Get out of here, call an Uber or whatever. I'll check in with you later, okay?

We've got to get these vamps out of the sun."

"Malik, you carry the familiar and I will follow with the North End. Quickly now."

The sensation of being lifted in strong, secure arms. *Dorchester*, he thought, and let himself drift away again. Wind in his face, but not one of his making. Searing heat to their right, just out of reach, threatening to consume their flesh if they didn't find shelter. His blood demon was restless, worried, but didn't resist Dorchester.

"I haven't lost my keys, thankfully." The metallic echo of Paul unlocking a door. "The lair is downstairs. Taviano, if you can hear me, I'm going to get everyone in your lair. Don't let your demon-thingy freak out, okay? We don't have time for its shit."

Feet pounding on stairs, the familiar scents of home. "Malik, can you open that vault door? It takes vamp strength, not my noodle arms."

Dorchester lowered him to his bed, still unmade from when the long, terrible evening began.

"Okay, you should be completely safe in here today. Taviano never lets me stay in case his bloodbeast takes me for a threat or a snack, so I guess it would be even riskier with three of you. Can I do anything for you during the day?"

"Yes," Dorchester answered. "Take this card please. It's my own familiar; the name is there. Call her and let her know what has happened and that I will be in touch at sunset."

"Will do. Malik, anything you need? No? Okay, you see the bar there. Close up shop, and I'll be waiting outside when you, uh, rise."

Taviano wanted to call out for Paul, to make him stay, but even in his dream state he knew that was a terrible and unwarranted risk. As the vault door closed and the bar fell into place, he gave himself over to the darkness.

NINETEEN

Paul

PAUL SANK DOWN against the barred door to the lair. Exhaustion crept over him but he needed to make sure Nonna and the others were safe.

Just a minute to rest, he told himself.

He looked at his hands, trying to find any signs of the strangeness he'd been through. They seemed normal now, no trace of the blue glow from earlier. The doctor vampire—and that was a trip to think about—had said the quintessence, whatever the fuck that was, had all come into him.

"At least Nonna won't get dragged further into this shit," Paul muttered. They still had a lot to talk about, though. He was sure, once the shock of the night had worn off, Nonna would be pissed that he'd kept so much from her.

Not that he knew how to explain. What had happened, when the light interfered to give Keres' essence to Taviano instead of that Russian fucker?

"I did that," Paul whispered. He had said it should be Taviano, and the light had made it happen. Was he magic now? Could he do cool shit?

He stood and looked around. A decorative candle sat on the table opposite the door to the lair. He squinted his eyes and thought at it, very hard. *Willed* it to move.

Nothing happened.

Fine, that would have been nifty, but fuck it. Maybe fire, like Taviano?

He stared again at the candle, eyes on the wick. He pictured a match, imagined it touching the wick, making it light.

Argh, still nothing.

"Try bigger," he muttered. He imagined heat rising in his body, and pictured a huge bonfire. Muscle strained as he put every bit of energy he could summon into making the god-dam…candle…Light!

The candle mocked him with its pristine, unlighted wick.

He strained and imagined and visualized for a half-hour, but none of the fantastic tricks he'd seen the vamps perform seemed to work for him.

Defeated for the moment, he drew from his pocket Keres' necklace. He'd swiped it after Bronislav did the world a favor. The metal charm was a bit sticky—*ewww, that's her ichor*—but he knew the image it represented was important.

Could ichor be the key to helping figure out if he was special now? With a grimace, Paul brought the charm to his lips, extended his tongue and licked the tiniest trace of ichor from the metal.

It tasted…dead. Nothing like when he drank in Taviano's ichor. Whatever power had once been in that shit on the charm, it was gone now.

Gone into Taviano.

Suddenly, the enormity of what he'd done hit Paul. "Oh God, please don't let me have fucked up," he muttered, putting his head in his hands.

Taviano had been struggling on and off for months with the memories and essences of the two vamps he'd absorbed. Keres was hella old, and obviously a lot more powerful than the chick that had tried to murder Paul at Christmas. Worse, Keres was a straight-up bitch, and cray-cray to boot.

What if Taviano couldn't handle so much power? What if it changed him somehow?

What if Taviano doesn't want me anymore?

The thought was unbearable. Taviano had become Paul's world in such a short span of time. It wasn't the gifts and the mansion and the wild sex. It was in the way Taviano believed in him, trusted him with huge responsibilities, showed Paul every day what he meant to Taviano.

"Coulda been this quintessence crap all along," he muttered aloud, then cringed. That was a shitty thing to think. He believed in three things absolutely.

Sunday Gravy was proof the Italians were the best cooks in the world.

Nonna was amazing and he'd spend his life trying to be as kick-ass as her.

And Taviano loved him.

Nodding to himself, Paul made his way upstairs and started making phone calls. Nonna sounded tired, but promised him she felt fine.

"I'm coming over later to make sure," Paul said.

"If you're coming, bring cookies. Or cheesecake would be even better."

Paul chuckled. "Got it, you greedy old woman. I'll stop by Bova's and pick some up."

"You sound tired, ragazzo. You should sleep. Whatever that was at the end, I think it took a lot out of you."

"Yeah, maybe you're right. I'll sleep a bit after I check in with the others, then come see you this afternoon. Taviano won't be back until six or so anyway."

She snorted into the phone. "Back, my ass. You've been lying to me, Paulie. He has to sleep by day, right? Your vampiro?"

"No more lies, Nonna. I promise."

After hanging up with Nonna, he checked on his cousins. Sofia was shaken but seemed okay. Luca started in on more questions about vampires and Paul had to cut him off.

"Come for Friendsgiving, day after Thanksgiving. Taviano will tell you anything you want to know."

Luca groaned. "You have a vampire boyfriend. Life goal, bro."

"It's pretty great. Aside from the kidnap thing tonight, but that's rare."

"You got killed once too, right?"

"Okay, that was another downside."

"And Taviano won't let you sleep in his lair with him, you said."

"I'm hanging up, Luca. You're a buzzkill."

That left one call, which he was both nervous and excited to make. God only knew what his father felt about the whole experience. It was traumatic, sure, but maybe it had opened his eyes, too? Maybe the possibility Paul might die, or Nonna, or Gianni himself, had made him think more about what was important?

The phone rang twice before his mother picked up.

"Mom? It's Paul."

There was a brief pause on the other end. "Oh. Paul." He heard her say as if over her shoulder, "It's Paul."

"Is Dad doing okay? Did he tell you about last night?"

"He said you're mixed up with some dangerous people. Your *boyfriend*"—he could hear distaste in the word—"is in a violent gang and a rival gang grabbed your father, your grandmother and your cousins for revenge. I told him we should call the police, but he doesn't want to draw attention to us. Paul, we raised you better than this."

"That isn't what happened!" Okay, except for the gang part, it was kind of what happened, but still. "Nonna, Luca and Sofia are all fine. I just wanted to see if Dad's all right. Can I talk to him?"

"He's resting. He doesn't want to come to the phone."

Paul winced, even though he had kind of expected that. He cast around, trying to think of something to say to show his mother that everything was fine. The pile of cookbooks with sticky flags for recipes he was considering caught his eye.

Some masochistic streak made him say, "Hey Mom? Nonna and a bunch of the cousins are coming over to my house the day after Thanksgiving. Maybe you and Dad would like to come so you can meet Taviano? You'll see he's not a gangster at all."

"I don't think so. We've made it clear we don't approve of your lifestyle, and last night shows that your choices have only grown more wrong and perverted."

"Mom—," he began, but there was a beep as she disconnected the call.

Paul stared at the phone in his hand. He waited to feel anger, or sadness, or something. But no, all he felt was resignation. If he'd had any remaining hope that time, or events, or the coming holidays would help heal their relationship, it was gone now.

He might as well be an orphan.

Brushing the back of his hand across his eyes, he climbed the stairs to his room and closed the door.

TWENTY

Taviano

T AVIANO DREAMED. NEARLY lost himself in nightmare. Fought his way back to the surface, to control. The things he saw in his mind were chaotic. Horrific. Terrifying.

Blinking eyes opened to see the astonished face of a hated man glaring down in horror, his hands still around her throat. The new thing in her head raked her hand across his face, gouging deeply. Blood welled and the thing was ravenous for it. She dragged the overseer down, crushing his bones as she lapped up the blood.

She was emerging from the sealed cargo area of her private jet. Her trusted aide had signaled that the sun was still hours from rising as it chased them West from Italy. Seating herself in the leather chair at her desk, she swiveled to watch the city lights spread below. Boston. If she was right, the answer was there somewhere. The mystery of the quintessence would be known at last, and she would take her place as first among the soul bearers that men called vampires.

It was the celebration of Bastille Day in Paris, some years after what was called the French Revolution. A perfect night for hunting, but it wasn't blood she needed. No, she'd heard of a soul bearer with the fire gift. Combined with her own power over water, this would give her mastery of two of the four elements. Even after these centuries, she couldn't find a pattern to which vampire progeny would manifest one of the elemental gifts. The guest in her own soul gave no guidance, though sometimes it let her know that it was ready to spread its influence through another mortal.

"Taviano?" Wonderful voice, so delightful. It tugged at him, bringing him forward for a moment. He almost had the name of the owner of that voice. It was on the edge of his thoughts... Then another memory surged and he sank again into Keres.

It was Italy again and she had only been returned to life a month ago. She girded herself for a struggle as she stood with her back to the wall of a house belonging to a wealthy Florentine merchant. With her perfect sight, she looked upon the faces of three others like her: A young boy, an old man, a woman. Each stood at a distance from the others, trembling with tension. The soul that lived in her knew the power residing within the others. They were repellent and yet she hungered to master them all, to compel all the soul bearers to bend to her will. And she knew they felt the same. The young boy had the look of a catamite, despite the fine clothes he now wore. He broke first, speeding away into the darkness. Her guest could track him until he was out of Florence. The old man tensed further and she prepared for an attack. When it came, she was ready. The battle was violent but brief. She was about to rip off his head when he managed to get free and run. The woman had remained still, watching the battle. She said, "This will be the way of it until the circle is squared." Then she, too, disappeared into the night.

Until the circle was squared? What had the woman meant?

"Babe, come back to me. Please." The voice he loved so much was sad. Distressed. Taviano wanted badly to comfort him. If he could just remember who the voice belonged to...

Keres was in the rooms of an aristocrat who fancied himself something of an alchemist but had lost his fortune. She had presented herself as a devotee and potential patroness, and suffered through his ramblings until he held up a charm. It was a circle encasing a triangle that itself contained a square with yet another circle inside. The guest in her soul sent a thrill of recognition. "Tell me of this," she had ordered too sharply, then had to soothe ruffled feathers before the alchemist would talk further. Unfortunately, everything he knew was mere superstition and vague references to Paracelsus, Cornelius Agrippa and back to Albertus Magnus from the thirteenth century. That gave her yet another shock. In modern parlance, she understood that she had been given this new, powerful life in the middle of the thirteenth century, though she had no way to identify a more precise year. The aristocrat quickly demonstrated the feeble limits of his knowledge. So she killed the fool, took the charm and his papers, and began to unravel the mystery of how to square the circle.

She closed a leather-bound tome with a feeling of satisfaction. The four elements of earth, air, fire and water, united and bound by the fifth element, the quintessence. That was the key, she was sure. Dangling her charm from one hand, she traced the center circle and the square that surrounded it. That much of the mystery made sense to her. The center represented the quintessence, and the four sides of the square were the four elemental gifts. The triangle, the outer circle, she was beginning to think they meant nothing, just ornamentation that had been added to the alchemical myth. She possessed two of the four gifts already. Her task must be to find soul bearers with the other two gifts and either gain their cooperation or take their essence for her own. And then this quintessence… That remained a mystery, but she had all the time in the world to solve it.

"Taviano, please wake up."

The sweet voice again, and this time lips pressed to his own. A scent filled his nostrils, the unmistakable essence of the man he loved. He inhaled deeply for pleasure, breathing in the musky body wash, the wonder that was—

"Paul."

He had to force his mouth to form the name, but as soon as

he did, it became an anchor. He voiced it again. "Paul."

"He said my name! That's it, babe. I'm Paul and I love you. Can you open your eyes for me?"

For Paul he could do anything, *dare* anything. Even as more of Keres' memories tried to drag him back, he blinked his eyes open. Blond hair, anxious cornflower-blue eyes, and the sweetest smile beamed down at him.

"Hello," he croaked, and managed a smile. Paul threw his head down against Taviano's shoulder, and Taviano's arms gently wrapped around the man he could feel sobbing and shuddering. "Paul, why are you crying?"

"You've been unresponsive for four nights." This was a woman's voice, coming from a small distance. Taviano rolled his head and found the source.

"Dorchester. Rani."

She nodded sharply. "Good. Do you feel the need for blood?"

Did he? Taviano shook his head. "No. The demon is too focused to want blood."

"Demon," Rani snorted. "So superstitious. Paul told me you once wanted to be a Catholic priest, so I suppose it makes sense."

Paul lifted his head, eyes wet and red. "I'm so sorry. I did this to you, didn't I? When I pushed Keres' ichor at you instead of Bratwurst."

"Bronislav," Taviano said, his mouth stretching into a slight grin. "Oh my love. Whatever it was you did when we were in battle—you saved me."

"And are you all right now?"

"I—I don't really know what's happening. The memories. Centuries, all over the place. No order to them. She was mad, delusional, egomaniacal. And I feel her beast still, trying to take control of mine."

"I believe that would be catastrophic for us all," Rani observed.

"No shit," came another voice. After a moment, Taviano remembered.

"Malik. Where are we?" He looked around, and it took time to realize they were all in his lair, underneath the house Paul called Castle Dracula.

Paul sat up and swiped a hand over his wet eyes. "I let them both come here that morning, when we needed to get away from the war zone. Rani and Malik have gone out when they needed to, but they came back to keep watch with me."

Others in his lair, with Paul. Alarm flared in Taviano.

"Are you all right?" he asked sharply, tensing as he glared at the two vampires. The surge of anguish forced Keres' essence away, giving him a brief respite in his battle with the vampire queen. If anyone had touched a hair on Paul's head...

"Chill, big guy," Paul said soothingly. "We're all on the same side. Nobody has even glanced at my neck." He made a mock punch to Taviano's shoulder. "And see? I was safe with you and with them. Ever since Malik reopened the lair that first night, I've stayed in here and tried to get you to wake up."

She was in a temple, stalking after the hierophant who belonged to a secret cult. He possessed a tome she needed...

Rani's voice helped drag him out of the memory. She sat in a chair, keeping a respectful distance. "It seemed to me that you responded to his voice, even if you couldn't come all the way out of your trance. I encouraged him to stay close, but Malik and I kept watch for any danger."

"Thank you," Taviano croaked out, and sank his head back down. Keres' essence surged again, threatening to take over his body and his mind. "Paul—"

"What do you need?" Paul asked anxiously. "Blood?"

Taviano shook his head no. That wasn't what his demon

wanted to master the powerful essence absorbed from the ancient vampire.

"I-I need you to be with me, Paul. Make love to me."

"And that's our cue to leave," Rani said. "Malik, you're welcome to follow me to Dorchester. I swear you'll be safe."

"Thank you," Malik answered with great formality. "If I can be of assistance to Dorchester, I will do so."

The two vampires departed quickly, Malik pausing long enough to move the crypt door mostly back into place, with enough room for Paul to slip in and out.

"They're gone," Paul said. Taviano could hear the tension in his voice. "Now, babe, tell me again what you want?"

"You are my anchor to humanity, my great love, my Paul. This heart knows that, as does the head. Keres is fighting to take over, but I think—I *hope*—that if you remind this body who it belongs to, my demon and I will be strong enough to resist her."

Paul was already shucking his clothes. "As come-ons go, I'd give that a six," he teased. "Good start, but the ending could have used a little more hearts and stars. Lucky for you I'm easy."

As soon as he was naked, he began to undress Taviano. In moments, Paul stretched to rest on top, skin to skin, and Taviano's arms curled around him protectively, lovingly. "Aaah," he sighed, the feel of Paul pulling him away from the maelstrom of Keres' memories. "You are a miracle."

They kissed hungrily, passion rising as Taviano left behind images of Florence in centuries past and came more firmly back to the modern world. Paul's excitement pressed against his thigh as they writhed, taking joy in each other. Paul slid down his body, bringing every nerve to life. He stroked a warm finger along Taviano's jaw and trailed down his neck. A twist of a nipple followed by a soothing lick brought a curse to Taviano's lips.

"Ooh, you'll have to confess that one next time you go to

Mass. Let's see if I can make the sins of the flesh worth the ten Hail Marys you'll have to do."

Then his warm mouth was on Taviano's member, readily willed to stiffness with his deep need. Paul bobbed his head, swiping his tongue across the large, flared head before sinking back down to take Taviano into his throat.

He came off it with a lascivious grin. "I can taste your precum already, baby. Strawberries today. You know how much I love the taste of ichor."

Taviano groaned. "And normally I would delight in giving you a mouthful of my essence. But I *need*—"

"I have you," Paul said soothingly. He moved lower, raising Taviano's knees and placing a kiss on either thigh. "Um, you know I haven't done this much, right? Topped, I mean?"

"Is it not what you want?" Taviano asked. "We don't have to—"

"No, no, bae. I want to." He took Taviano's hand and wrapped it around his own penis, hard as a rock. "I *really* want to. I'm just worried it won't be good for you."

"Every way you touch me is good. I know you as my gentle and passionate lover, and I want to give you pleasure always. If there's a better way for us to make love, I can't imagine it."

"Okay, that brought your come-on up to a solid eight." Paul reached to the bedside table and pulled out a bottle of lubricant. The snick of the top opening echoed in the quiet, intimate lair.

Paul poured a generous amount into his palm, then swiped it along his shaft with a hiss. "Uh, should I prep you, babe?" he asked, teasing a slick finger along Taviano's opening.

"No, please. You can't really hurt me, and even if there's a brief pain it will help anchor me in the here and now." Taviano pulled back his legs, hooking arms under knees. "I want you so much."

Paul shifted until the head of his member pressed against Taviano, and slowly applied pressure. Taviano tensed in spite of himself; the discomfort was more than he'd expected. The flare of pain caused a slip of his consciousness and Keres once more grappled for dominance. Taviano silently asked his demon for help, and immediately felt a change within his undead body. He relaxed, allowing Paul to slip inside him. The sensation of being filled was so profound, so immediate, that he again pushed Keres down into submission.

Paul had paused to measure how Taviano was reacting, but there was no longer any need to go slow. "You feel wonderful, my love. Don't worry, it doesn't hurt."

Sliding his full length into Taviano's body, Paul bent for a kiss, the move pressing him even deeper. A pleasant pressure made Taviano's own penis jump, and ichor drip out onto his belly. "Oh!" he exclaimed. "Is that my prostate?"

Paul grinned as he withdrew, then angled to sink in again, once more bringing that extra thrill of pleasure. "Now I get to show you why I'm such a slut when you're fucking me."

Taviano pulled his legs back further, giving Paul complete access. Keres' essence had grown more feeble, its resistance fading away. Paul in his body, soul calling to soul, flesh to flesh… His blood spirit drew on all those sensations to weave the remnants of Keres into its own shape.

Heartened, Taviano teased back. "Do your worst, fiend." Experimentally, he flexed muscles inside himself that made Paul gasp.

"Do that again and this'll be over before you know it." Paul swiveled his hips, grinding himself wonderfully inside. "I had no idea how much I'd enjoy being on this end of things."

"You can do this to me anytime you want. You can do *anything*. I trust you completely."

"Yeah? So you like"—Paul increased his tempo—"that, too?"

Taviano groaned with pleasure and nodded, rocking himself to take Paul to new depths. The connection left no room for Keres. He and his blood spirit were winning.

"Will you say it for me?" Paul asked, grinning. "You know how much I like to talk dirty when you're fucking me. Tell me what you like."

"I love your c-cock, Paul. It's stroking inside me just perfectly. Making my, my ass feel pleasure."

Paul increased his pace again. "That's it, babe. Who does your body belong to?"

"It belongs to you. I belong to you, completely."

And it was true. It had worked. The physical connection united his mind, his body and his heart, giving him the strength to force Keres' insanity into a corner of his blood spirit's complete shape. He couldn't yet assess what absorbing Keres had done to his strength and powers, but with Paul's help, his body was his own once more.

"Oh, like that," Taviano moaned. "So good when you fu-fuck me."

Paul entwined Taviano in his arms, crushing their bodies together tightly as his hips thrust and withdrew. Taviano released the hold on his knees to wrap his legs around Paul's back and hold onto Paul's ass, pulling him in relentlessly. Taviano was dimly aware that the demon was enjoying the lovemaking, too.

The swelling pleasure of impending orgasm began, drawing tension like the ebb of a tide, building energy for when it reversed, surging back higher and higher into an unstoppable wave.

"I'm gonna come," Paul gasped, his thrusts deliberately slowing as he tried to delay the moment, to prolong his pleasure. He groaned as he withdrew with exquisite care until only the head remained inside Taviano. Then Paul cried out and thrust back inside all at once.

The pleasure inside Taviano crested and crashed throughout his body. He could feel each throb of Paul's orgasm, could feel the precious fluid coating his insides, the warmth it brought with it. Ichor came out of his own member in spasm after spasm, coating both their bellies as they writhed.

They panted together, holding each other close. "Holy shit. That was amazing," Paul gasped, letting himself sink onto Taviano with his full weight.

Taviano kissed the side of his head, nudging with his nose until Paul met him in another languid kiss. They lay together, almost one body. Keres was conquered, and the demon inside Taviano curled up in satisfaction, like a cat in the sun.

Gradually, Paul tensed. Eventually he raised himself on one elbow, resting his head on his fist. Concern darkened his eyes. "Taviano, can I ask you something? Are...?" He blew out a breath that lifted his bangs briefly. "Are you positive you love me? No, I'm sorry I asked. I'm one hundred percent sure you do. But these days you were unconscious... I couldn't help wondering about what it all means. What if your beastie just forced you to be with me because I'm some kind of Cracker Jack prize for it?"

Taviano stroked a few stray strands of hair out of Paul's face. "I worried about something similar for a time, until I saw your eyes after the battle. Did the demon manipulate us for its own ends? Likely. But as to love, I think... Yes, I think I've got answers for us both." He rolled them over so his hand was under Paul's shoulder and Paul relaxed back onto the bed. Leaning down, he tenderly kissed the tattoo of a sunrise on Paul's chest.

"I present my case. First, apparently this quintessence, whatever that means, was not solely within you but in other members of your family, correct? Well, I can assure you that I feel deep affection and respect for your grandmother, but I definitely don't love her or want to do this with her."

"Gross," Paul grinned despite the worry in his eyes. "Not to be ageist or anything, but she's my *nonna*!"

"If you want to be technical, sweetheart, she's closer to my age than you are."

"Yeah, but you're still, like, a century older than her. So you'd be a cradle robber either way, you perv."

"Noted. May I proceed? Second, your family seems to like me well enough when we've met, although tonight might understandably cool their friendliness. Yet none of them seem overcome with love and passion for me."

"Whereas I fell into bed with you in about ten minutes. Overcome." Paul snorted. "Cocky much?"

"Only where it relates to you, my love. Point Three, I've been in Keres' memories. She looked at you and your family as a human might look at a collection of…I don't know. Horses, perhaps. To her, you were interesting and potentially useful, but not objects of love."

"Whereas you want to jump on this horse and ride him into the sunset. Admit it," Paul giggled, tickling Taviano's ribs.

"I confess you are the only horse for me," Taviano said solemnly. "We could get you a saddle, and some hooves, perhaps a tail—"

"Oo, pony play. I've read about that!"

"Wait, you mean humans actually do that? Pretend to be a horse and a, well, a cowboy? As a sexual act?"

"I think so. We'll have to do some porn research one of these long winter nights coming up."

"Back to the point." Taviano kissed Paul's nose. "Four, my blood spirit finally answered me directly when I demanded to know if it had forced us to care for each other. It denies that completely, and now I believe it, demon though it may be. And thus I rest my case. My love for you is completely my own. Do you have any rebuttal or contrary evidence to enter into the record?"

"No more *Law & Order* reruns for you, counselor," Paul said, reaching up to stroke his fingers through Taviano's hair. "But you've convinced me. I didn't feel anything for all those other vamps tonight." A twinkle returned to his eye. "Though Rani is pretty hot. And a doctor to boot."

"Maybe, but does she have a castle? I don't think so."

Paul laughed, "Okay. You love me for realsies. I love you to the moon and back. But what do we think about this quintessence fuckery?"

"The jury—meaning my demon—is still out on that. Let me tell you about some of the things I gleaned from Keres' memories."

TWENTY-ONE

Paul

AFTER TAVIANO SEALED himself back in the lair for the day, Paul came upstairs. With his vampire in a stupor, Paul had lost track of the calendar. The humongous television in the den was playing and the first thing he saw on it was the Macy's Thanksgiving Day parade.

"Oh hell, I totally forgot about shopping and prep for Friendsgiving!"

He rushed to find his phone, cursed when he saw it was dead, and fumbled around to find a charge cord. Once the screen lit up again, he saw he'd missed several messages. The first one he returned was from Nonna.

"Sorry I missed your call," he blurted as soon as she answered, "but I've been with Taviano."

"Is he doing well?" The words were kind but there was an edge to Nonna's question that put Paul on his guard.

"He is. I mean, we still haven't figured out what this quintessence shit is all about, but we think we have a place to start."

"So. My news. I got an earful from Gianni about that night, and about your call the next day. And that they were refusing to go to your Friendsgiving. I told Gianni that if he didn't appreciate that his son and his son's lover had saved his life, then the point of the day was wasted on him and I wasn't going to spend Thanksgiving with him."

"You didn't!' Paul gasped.

"I did. He's my only son, but you're my only grandson. Between the two, I know who is the better man." Paul could hear the tears creeping into her voice. "I must be to blame somehow, but I don't know where I went wrong with him."

"Oh, Nonna, I can't believe you did anything wrong. It's just life, and circumstance, and who he knew and hung around with."

She blew her nose away from the phone. When she spoke again, her voice was stronger. "Anyway. I'm sure you haven't had time to think about food for your Friendsgiving event. But would you and Taviano like to come have Thanksgiving dinner with me? I already invited Luca and Sofia and some of your other cousins. It's all on a message I left on your phone."

"That sounds wonderful, Nonna. Um, if it isn't too much, could I also bring Malik and Rani? They're the other two, uh—"

"Vampiri."

"Yeah, vampires from the other night. They stayed with me and Taviano until he woke up. I know Malik doesn't have anyone. Not sure about Rani."

"Of course. We're Italians. The more mouths to feed, the happier I am. What time can the bloodsuckers all come out safely?" Nonna asked with a cackle.

"You aren't going to call them that tonight, are you?"

"Of course not. Pensi che io sia scortese?"

"No, I don't think you're rude," Paul said, doubtfully.

"My phone says sunset is about four-fifteen. I'll have the humans come earlier, but bring the vampiri anytime. Ne mangeremo circa sei." A pause, and then she added, "But warn your Taviano. I'm going to have a few words for him first."

That evening, after checking that Malik and Rani had something to pretend to eat or drink, Paul dragged Taviano by the hand over to his grandmother. She sat in her rocking chair, white hair pulled back into a tight bun, shrewd eyes narrowed at the man she'd just recently learned was a vampire.

"Nonna, I wanted to tell you for so long," Paul said, hoping to preempt whatever she intended to say. "I just didn't know how without sounding crazy. Or, you know, being told I'm an idiot for getting mixed up with a bloodsucking monster." He winked at Taviano. "No offense, babe."

"None taken," Taviano said in his deep voice. Cautiously, he extended a hand to Nonna. "I feel as though we should meet all over again, now that you know who and what I am."

Nonna just sat there, ignoring the outstretched hand. She rocked slowly, deliberately. Silently.

Taviano cleared his throat, then tried again. "I'm glad you're safe. Thank you for everything you did to save Paul. He is a remarkable man and I believe it is because of you."

Paul felt himself start to sweat. Nonna had a right to be pissed, sure, but he wanted her to love Taviano as much as he did. Nervously he jabbered, "Taviano's the same man you met and liked before, Nonna. It's just he also is super powerful and drinks blood. But you know it was Taviano who got me managing the work on the shelter. He told me I could do it and I think he's right. And there's so much more I couldn't tell you about before. He's the best man I've ever met. You won't believe the shit he's got me doing with his money, the places we give it anonymously. Please, Nonna. Please be nice to him."

Nonna stopped rocking. Gnarled hands gripped the arms of her rocker as she pushed herself to her feet. Taviano shot a quick glance his way, then looked back at his tiny grandmother.

She took three steps closer to Taviano and came to a stop, looking up up *up* his tall body. She crooked her finger for

Taviano to bend down, and Paul heaved a sigh of happiness. It was going to be all right. She'd kiss Taviano, welcome him, maybe scold him for putting her grandson in danger...

"Taviano Adelfio," Nonna hissed into his boyfriend's face. Then she hauled off and slapped him.

"Wait. What?" Paul gasped. Taviano reeled back, shock on his face as he raised a hand to cover the mark she'd left on his cheek. "Nonna, what are you doing?"

"That," she hissed at Taviano, "is for my grandfather Calogero. He believed his whole adult life that he was responsible for the death of his closest friend. And here you are, looking beautiful as sin and young as my Paulie. Come osi?"

The surprise and confusion on Taviano's face as he looked down at a dynamo half his size, reading him, was so comical it almost made Paul snort despite his own shock. "Uh, Nonna," he said cautiously, "what are you talking about?" at the same time Taviano blurted out, "Calogero blamed himself for my death?"

"Of course he did." Nonna all but spit the words. "Always he carried guilt and sadness with him in his back pocket. On the most joyous days, I still knew it was there. Christmas was the worst. Some years he couldn't even leave the house to go to Christmas Mass. All he would say then is, 'Taviano loved Christmas so much.'

"I finally got the story out of him, shortly before he died. 'Conchetta,' he said to me, 'I turned my back on my best friend when he needed me most, right before I married your grandmother. Taviano, his name was. Taviano Adelfio. He and I, we were close. Maybe too close. When I turned him away, he took his own life.'"

"But I didn't," Taviano protested. "The last night I talked to Calogero, I left him just to get drunk. And that was the same night Bronislav took me," he added more slowly, nodding his head. Understanding bloomed in his face. "Of course Calogero thought I died that night. He knew I never would have left Naples voluntarily without saying goodbye, and he had no reason to guess I was forced away. So he assumed I took my own life, because of him."

"But that isn't what happened," Paul protested. "Nonna, the bad dude who grabbed us before, the Russian one. He turned Taviano into a vampire and made him leave Naples. He had no way to say goodbye or explain to anyone."

"I did look for Calogero," Taviano said earnestly. "Years after that night, when I was finally free, I returned to Naples. I wanted to see him and my own family, to tell them I was all right, to learn how they were. But my parents were in the cemetery and I found no one who could tell me where Calogero had gone."

Nonna narrowed her eyes, weighing Taviano's words. She glanced over at Paul, then back at Taviano. "Were you and my grandfather in love?" she demanded.

Taviano swallowed but didn't take his eyes away from her. "We were lovers of sorts, but Calogero was never *in* love with me, not really. I...I thought I was in love with him." He turned to Paul and extended a hand. Paul stepped into his embrace as Taviano said to Nonna, "I didn't know what love was, until I met Paul. What I felt for your grandfather was a pale shadow of what I have now."

"Taviano," Paul sighed, and rested their foreheads together. "I love you, too."

"Okay," Nonna said, shrugging broadly with her hands raised.

"Um. Okay?" Paul asked tentatively as she turned away and started toward the small sideboard in her apartment.

"Yes, okay. An old man felt guilt all his life, but your *vampiro* didn't do that to him. He loves you, and you tell me he has a good heart. So it's okay that you're together. Who wants wine?"

. . .

A FEW HOURS later, with the meal finished, Luca took charge of some of the younger cousins to begin cleanup. The rest lounged around Nonna's crowded dining room table. Rani murmured that she needed to leave soon because she was on shift at the hospital. Malik was talking with Sofia about whether and how he could approach his own parents. Paul heard him say, "I know I don't look like I used to. My eyes, even my skin have changed color, enough that they'll know."

Paul cleared his throat and tapped a fork against his wine glass. "Before we scatter, can I say something?"

Everyone turned their attention to him. Luca peeked in from the kitchen.

"I know some really weird shit has happened"—(from the kitchen he heard a young voice giggle, *He said 'shit'! Ow, Uncle Luca!*)—"and we don't understand it all. But we got through it, working together. Helping each other. Humans, vampires, the demon thingies in your bodies." (*What's cousin Paulie talking about? Vampires? Uncle Luca, quit hitting me, I was just asking!*) "We lived through it. So I want to raise a glass to all of us, the Fang Gang, and give thanks for you being in my life. In *our* lives," he amended, taking Taviano's hand.

Everyone clinked their glasses and drank. Even Malik, Rani and Taviano took small sips of the wine.

Setting down his glass, Taviano said, "While we're gathered, perhaps someone here has an insight into the things I saw in Keres' memories." He explained about the images he could decipher from the chaos of the dead vampire's mind, all the way back to her death and rebirth in the thirteenth century.

When he paused, Nonna said with mounting excitement.

"That's an interesting coincidence. Ma forse non è una coincidenza!"

"What isn't a coincidence?" Paul asked.

She lapsed entirely into Italian, excited about some insight. "Alora, questa situazione vampiro ebbe inizio a Firenze, vero? Nel tredicesimo secolo?"

"English, Aunt Conchetta," Sofia chided gently. "Yes, it started in Florence in the thirteenth century."

"Mi dispiace, yes, English. And there was a baby, right? Well, you know who was born in Florence in 1265?"

Everyone shook their head. Paul could see the glint in Nonna's eye, the excitement in her bearing, so typical of her when she used to teach English.

"I'll tell you who. Dante Alighieri."

Malik chimed in. "The guy who wrote *The Inferno*?"

"If I still had gold star stickers, I'd give you one," Nonna said proudly.

Malik put his hands over his cheeks. "I read *The Inferno* last year in Comparative Lit. It's about the nine circles of Hell and all the types of sinners who are being punished in each level."

Taviano gasped. "Alighieri. The tree on Paul's back! My love, where did you get the image of the tree you used? Did you design it yourself?"

"What tree are we talking about?" Sofia asked.

"It's a tat. I'll show you." Paul hiked up his shirt and turned around, letting everyone see his ink. A huge spreading tree covered half of Paul's back, one small section left to show a broken branch representing the estrangement from his parents. "I sketched it out myself and took it to the tattoo place where I got my sunrise. It just seemed right."

"I think it's a *family* tree you felt compelled to draw," Taviano said with certainty. He gestured to the crown of the design.

"If this is you, Paul, then this lopped off bit, er…" He fumbled to a stop, glancing at Nonna.

"Gianni and his wife," she said in a level voice. "Continua."

"Prego. Then this forked branch might be you, Nonna, and your sister Carla." He trailed down a bit. "And this would be about right for—"

"Calogero Alighieri!" Paul shouted. "And if my great-whatever-nonno was an Alighieri…"

Taviano rested a palm against the root of the tree image. "Then perhaps he was a descendant of *Dante* Alighieri."

Sofia shook her head. "You can't seriously be suggesting that this, this…quintessence"—she gestured casually at herself and the others who had been in the basement cell—"has somehow lingered and followed in a line of descent reaching back *seven hundred fifty years* to the poet Dante?"

Malik shrugged. "Well, I'm not. But I'm not going to say it can't be true. After all, I don't know how this is possible either." The glass figurine of a cat on Nonna's breakfront sagged into a glob, then reformed itself into a prism.

"You'll put that back before you leave, young man," Nonna chided, getting a subdued "yes'm" in reply.

Paul lowered his shirt and took his seat again. He leaned his elbows on the table and then put his chin on his fists. "I guess we'll never know for sure, but what a trip that is, to think we're connected like that. Who needs more cheesecake?"

Rani tilted her head quizzically. "Yes, it's unsettling and we've gotten through it so far. But Paul, you make it sound like you think everything is over."

"Oh, well, isn't it? That Keres bitch is dead," Paul said firmly.

"But the images that we all saw that night." She indicated Taviano, Malik and herself. "The message that went out didn't stop with us. I've heard calls and rumblings from other vampires in Massachusetts already, and some of them have heard from vampires as far away as Ireland and Libya. I think it's a safe guess that the images reached every vampire. Now, I doubt they know what it means any more than we do, or where it came from." She shook her head ruefully. "But I can't agree that it's over. I think that was not just a message that the five of you inadvertently sent out to us, but a summons to all."

Paul felt the blood draining from his face.

From the doorway, Luca muttered, "Way to kill the mood. And after I let you drink from me, too."

Rani smiled affectionately at him. "You were very tasty. I don't mean to bring the room down, or alarm anyone unduly. I just believe we should consider and prepare for what might be coming. It seems some of our kind see control of the quintessence as a way to dominate us all. Keres is gone, but Bronislav is not. And he knows quite a bit about this, perhaps more than we know. It stands to reason more will come to try to claim or kill Paul, now that he is the sole bearer of the quintessence."

"Well, shit," Taviano said with a growl.

Paul turned to him, mouth open, momentarily distracted by the swear. "There you go, babe! Cursing like a modern-day mortal. We'll bring you up to date in no time."

Taviano ruffled his hair. "I'll keep working on my potty mouth, just for you. But I hate that you might still be in danger. I just can't understand what is going on."

"Me neither," Luca sighed from the kitchen, dish towel and dried roasting pan in his hand. "But *man* your life is cool, Paulie."

"We'll figure it out, though," Taviano added reassuringly, resting a hand on Paul's knee. "I've tried to protect you, but you have a power of your own now. Whatever it is, you were able to knock Bronislav into a wall, and you saved me from Keres' control with just your love. Whatever this summons means, it affects all of us in this room in one way or another, and we will figure it out together."

True enough, Paul thought.

He looked around the assemblage for this unexpected Friendsgiving. Some were family he'd known all his life. Some were vampires, possessed by supernatural beings that might be demons or soul guests or bloodbeasts. One in particular was the best person he'd ever known, alive or dead. He had lost a family when his parents rejected him for who and what he was. But in these assembled humans, vampires and demons, he'd found a more loving and powerful family to see him through whatever was to come.

Even if it was to be a war with the undead.

THE END...FOR NOW

Paul and Taviano's story will conclude in HOLIDAYS SUCK! part 3, coming soon!

Thank you for reading *Fangsgiving*. I hope your holidays are smoother than Taviano and Paul's, and that you will want to see what this vampire and his human get up to in Part 3 of the HOLIDAYS SUCK! trilogy, coming soon!

If you did enjoy the book, **please consider leaving a review** on Amazon, Goodreads, TikTok, or other sites that discuss MM romance. I appreciate any feedback, no matter how long or short. It's a great way to let other romance fans know what you thought about this book. Being an independent author means that every review really does make a huge difference, and I'd be grateful if you take a minute to share your opinion with others.

About the Author

Robert Winter lives and writes in Provincetown. He is a recovering lawyer who prefers writing about hot men in love much more than drafting a legal brief. He left behind the (allegedly) glamorous world of an international law firm to sit in his home office and dream up ways to torment his characters until they realize they are perfect for each other.

When he isn't writing, Robert likes to cook Indian food and explore new restaurants.

Contact Robert at the following links:

Website:
www.robertwinterauthor.com

Facebook:
facebook.com/robert.winter.921230

Goodreads:
goodreads.com/author/show/16068736.Robert_Winter

TikTok:
@robertwinterauthor

Email:
RobertWinterAuthor@comcast.net

29500107R00093